ALSO BY ANTHONY MINGHELLA

Jim Henson's
"THE STORYTELLER"

Jim Henson's
"THE STORYTELLER"

by Anthony Minghella

Illustrations by Darcy May

Alfred A. Knopf   *New York*   1991

Contents

NONE of the nine stories in this book is my own. I have plundered and borrowed from the riches of the European folktale and extracted those narratives which seemed beautiful or strange or delightful without the burden of scholarship to restrain me. These stories have been told and repeated through the ages, changing with each retelling, so that every country and culture has its own set of variants on the classic tales. I have felt like a man who hears a good joke and tells it to his friends. I have taken liberties, invented what I have forgotten, and changed what I have remembered. At the same time, I have tried not to impose my own judgment on the material. Italo Calvino, in his marvelous anthology of *Italian Folktales,* described himself as a link in the anonymous chain without end by which folktales are handed down. I am happy to join him, guided by the same Tuscan proverb he invoked for his own work: "The tale is not beautiful if nothing is added to it."

This book is for my son Max, who began his life as I began these stories. I have tried to fill his days with their magic just as he has filled my days with his own.   A.M.

Jim Henson's
"THE STORYTELLER"

The
Three
Ravens

HERE was once a kingdom where all was happy, where flowers grew, where songs were sung. And in this kingdom a good King reigned and loved and was cherished. What he gave he got back tenfold, for there were rich harvests, golden days, and children. And his Queen was a woman of wit and majesty, of great grace. Her smile was passed from mouth to mouth in the country like a gift. Which it was. Her smile blessed the land and what it touched grew, what it touched was healed.

Then, one bleak day in November, the Queen died. Outside the palace, the leaves fell lamenting, reds and golds, falling. Inside, at the end of the Great Hall, in the long shadows, the King, his three sons, and his daughter stood weeping. And the people filed slowly by, hour after hour, to shed their own tears for the dear Queen.

But there was one among the mourners whose eyes were dry, whose brain raced ahead to the day when the King would want to ease his loneliness. And the Witch, for Witch she was, swept her cold gaze across the solemn faces, the sorrow and the sadness, lingered icily on the Princess and her three brothers, then fixed her dry eyes on the King. And schemed. A simple, terrible scheme. She groaned for power, for majesty over all things, for the cold ring of gold around her head. She wanted this until the want ate away her heart and soul. So

she set to work on the King. As the days passed on their slow march, she inched her way into his life.

At first the King didn't even see the Witch, didn't feel the sun on his face, or the rain. Just the tug of the past, all day, all night, memories tugging on his sleeve. His poor heart was broken. But the Witch could charm the skin from a snake, the leaves from the trees, and she turned all her power on the King. She wound him in, the past tugging him one way, she patiently pulling him the other.

One day she crept upon him, hunched and broken over his wife's tomb, flowers in his hand, flowers on the grave. As he shivered, he felt a cloak surround him. And, pulling it to his breast, he turned and saw the Witch standing before him, all concern, all kindness. How strange he felt. And shaken. Because for an instant when he looked at her he thought he saw his wife's darling face. And indeed he did. For the Witch had enchanted him. Her own hard beauty blurred into the soothing features of the lamented Queen. It was a spell. And it worked. "You're back," he kept saying. And the Witch replied, "Our little secret."

So it began, the King wanting to feast forever on the Witch, the Witch reeling him in. One day they walked together, one day he held her hand, one day he kissed her. How happy he imagined he was! He called together his children, their eyes still red from weeping. The Witch was with him. He introduced her. His eyes could not leave her as he spoke. "Children, I have something wonderful to tell you. I'm going to be married. We're going to be happy again." The Witch smiled at them. "I hope you'll think of me as your friend," she said, "and then—in time—as your mother."

"Our mother's dead," they said, huddling together. "New mother," said the King quickly. "I think we mean as a new mother." "That's right," said the Witch. "In time." Then she went, sweeping out. Behind her, in the room, the four children stood, threatened and bewildered, while their father hugged them to him, hugged and hugged, begging them to try, begging them to understand. And as they hugged, they nodded somberly, promising to try. All hugs, all family, but the Witch watched from outside—and cursed them. They were her rivals and her enemies. Because she would not share. She wanted it all. She married the King and darkened the smile on the land to a scowl where shadows set and nothing would grow in them.

And the Witch sowed a seed of fear in the children's lives. Stairs gave way, horses bucked wild, balconies crumbled. The world was dangerous. . . . One day, a toy box was full of snakes, hissing and writhing. Another day, the Princess put on the necklace that had been her mother's and felt it tighten and tighten around her neck. Terror whispered its threat through the palace. Of course the Witch herself was all honey, always honey, but sometimes the King caught her chill look and worried she was also the bee. And could sting.

Whenever he did, the sharp features would soften and beguile him. But now each time it took longer. Poor man, then. Torn in half. Enchanted by his new Queen, frightened for his children. What could he do?

The King had a magic ball of twine. It knew its way through the forests. Roll it into the trees and it would pick the path, this way and that, to where a secret cottage lay, pink and perfect. Here were streams and sanctuary. The King lay awake one dark night beside the Witch, watched her thin cold sleep, and decided. Next morning, he slipped from the bed, roused the children, and took them quickly to the edge of the forest. From his cloak he fetched the magic twine and set it rolling. For an hour they followed its marvelous journey, saying nothing, past glade and glen, this way and that, until they came to a clearing and saw before them the cottage. Sorrow slipped from their shoulders, for their mother's smile lived here still and warmed them.

"It's perfect!" they agreed, and embraced each other, clapping backs, delighted. The boys larked and larruped as if a great weight had lifted off them. And the Princess, their sister, sat by the stream and dipped her toes and missed her mother, which she always did when she was happy.

"This is our secret place," said the King gently, sitting down beside her, taking her hand in his. "Secret from all the world. No one can find you here." The Princess gazed at the stream, not looking at her father. "You've brought us here because of her, haven't you?" she said. "Our stepmother." And though the King protested, and though he would not admit it, she was right. He had.

As they spoke, the Witch, her stepmother, sat in her gray tower and studied horrible spells. The children were obstacles between her and power, growing, daily growing like clouds over her. Now she would catch these clouds, and puff them clean away. All night she brewed, all night she recited, all night she cursed her dark curses. When, next day, the King returned to the palace and sought her out, he found her spinning at the wheel, sending black threads of silk to and fro, her scowl stretched into a smile as sharp as a bee's sting.

"Where've you been?" she inquired, all honey. And as the King explained he'd taken the children on a holiday, she nodded; as he said "special," she nodded. Oh yes, she understood everything. Did he like her sewing? she wondered. She was sewing shirts, she said, sewing them all little shirts. The King felt terrible. He'd misjudged his new Queen. There she was at home sewing presents for his children while he was hiding them away from her. The Witch pinched him. "You're being very mysterious," she teased. "Where are the children? Our children? You want me to be the mother, but what mother can tolerate not knowing where her children have gone?"

Suddenly the King was uneasy again. "I wanted them to have a secret holiday. It makes it special." The Witch laughed. A cackle. "Secret," she said, cackling again. "Of course. But what if something should happen to you? Then what would we do? Or happen to them?" She bit into the thread, snapping it. "Still. Let that be an end to it. You don't want to tell me. It's your right. They're your children. I am only the stepmother." And, saying this, she spun the wheel and left him there to watch it turn and turn and turn.

Whatever her words, the Witch had no intention of letting that be an end to it. The next day when the King rode off to visit the children, she followed, stealthy as a bat, and watched him roll out the magic thread, watched its magic twists and turns, smiled her beesting smile. That night while the King slept, she searched for the twine, sly and silent, rummaging and rooting, willing it to appear. And she found the twine and stole it, and in its place left a ball of common thread. Then off at first light to find the poor children, her enemies, carrying with her magic thread and magic shirts and magic curses.

Morning found the three Princes knee deep in the stream, tickling for trout. Every now and then a cry would break the silence, a shout and a laugh as a wriggling fish would leap from grasping hands and splash back on its way. Nearby, in the forest, the Princess wandered, gathering lilies and primroses, full of joy, hearing her brothers' yelps and hoots of pleasure. The children had not known such peace for a long time. Fish came and flowers, and they were delighted.

A little way off, at the edge of the forest, the Witch, their stepmother, rolled out the magic ball of twine and hurried after it. As she disappeared into the thick and fast, the King arrived to visit his children, pulled out his ball of thread, and threw it onto the ground, where it stayed, stubborn, stock-still. He picked it up and cast it down again, but nothing. It would not move. The King was first dumbfounded, next aggravated; then slowly, dawning, he felt an unease, a disquiet that spread and grew and filled him with terror. He abandoned the useless thread and began to run, run into the heart of the forest.

The three Princes ran into the house, full of victory, their net bulging with fish to cook for supper. Their father would be proud of them. They carried the heaving catch into the pantry. Sitting there, shrouded in black, skin like marble, cold eyes gleaming, was the Witch. "Have you caught these fish yourselves?" she asked, all innocence, as if her presence were the most natural thing in the world. "How clever!" she said. The boys moved together and back a step. "How did you find us?" they asked. "And where's our father?"

The Witch produced her most soothing voice. Treacle. She moved toward them, explaining that their father was on his way—why didn't she cook the fish for them? Would they like to see the presents she'd made? Special presents? . . . And with this she produced the shirts, held them up, their black silk sleeves fluttering like wings. "I sewed each one by hand. Aren't they nice? Try them on. Then your father can see them. Your fish, my shirts—we'll surprise him." Her voice sang, singsong, treacly. The boys took the shirts and shivered. The Witch barely watched as they changed from their tunics. Instead, her eyes fixed on the window toward the forest. "And where's your sister?" she sang. "I miss her. I miss her."

The Princess was strolling in the forest, her arms brushing branches, calm and carefree. She heard the birds singing, the trees sighing. She could not hear her father's anxious calls as he wandered lost and bewildered in the heart of the forest.

In the cottage, her brothers tied the ribbons of their shirts, buttoned up the necks. The Witch turned to them, beesting smile. She began to mutter. An incantation, a low rhythmic verse, over and over, faster and faster, louder and louder. And this is what she said:

> The shirts will hurt, the wings will sting,
> the beaks will shriek, the eyes will cry.
> The shirts will hurt, the wings will sting,
> the beaks will shriek, the eyes will cry.
> The shirts will hurt, the wings will sting,
> the beaks will shriek, the eyes will cry.

And as her curse grew louder, booming through the cottage, the terrible shirts tightened on the young boys, pulled and tightened like skin around them, shredding and squeezing, ripping into tatters. They looked at themselves in terror, fearful of the Witch, her cruel voice winding round them, pulling. What was happening to them? Their shirts hurt, their arms felt like wings, stinging them, their eyes blinked back tears; and from their own mouths came shrieks. Awful, awful. They were turning into birds, they were turning into Ravens, swirling in the room, blind, panicked. Out they flew, out, out, away from the Witch's triumphant screams.

The Princess saw them as she returned toward the cottage, her basket full of flowers. The Ravens circled over her, shrieking and shrieking, terrified. She dropped her basket and ran toward the open door of the cottage, then stopped dead in her tracks when she saw the

Witch at the window, staring, willing her in. The Princess turned and fled for her life, losing shoe and shawl, the Witch pursuing her, a black bat with arms outstretched, possessed. Ravens above her, shrieking.

At the very instant his daughter disappeared into the forest's embrace, the King finally found his way out of its labyrinth. There was the Queen, his wife, the Witch, hurtling from the house, wild in her triumph, the path strewn with flowers and discarded garments, feathers everywhere, anguished cries of "Father! Father!" ringing in his ears. "What have you done?" he roared at the Witch. "Me?" she replied, pulling up and oozing honey. "I've done nothing."

But the King would have none of it. His voice was stern. "I ask you again, what have you done with my children?" His wife was all innocence, amazed. "Are the children here?" As she spoke, her face melted into the features of the dead Queen. The King covered his eyes with his hands, trying not to look at her. She willed him to, willed him to, but he would not. "My boys!" he cried, desperate. The three Ravens circled above them. "My boys! My daughter! Where are they? I heard my daughter cry out to me!"

The Witch's face relaxed, returned, her smile a curved sneer of ice. She whispered, she cooed. "I think you must be unwell. Are you sickening for something? Let me see. Let me soothe you." But the spell on the King was broken and he pushed her roughly to the ground. A hiss came from her lips. She looked up at him, her cruelty plain and unmasked. "Yes, you're upset," she hissed ominously. "I'll have to think about this. About what we can do with you." Then she picked up one of the lilies the Princess had gathered and fixed on it. The King stared, astounded, as the flower drooped in her grip and wound itself round her fist as a spitting, evil snake. It was the last thing he saw before the snake leapt onto his neck and began its bitter caress.

For a day and a night the Princess ran, stumbled, fled until she dropped into a dead sleep, and when she woke, she saw three Ravens before her, or perhaps she dreamed it, because they spoke to her. "Sister," they seemed to say. "Listen to us. We are your brothers. She did this to us. We are trapped. Help us. Help us. You must keep silent. You must not speak to a single soul for three years, three months, three weeks, and three days. Only then can the spell be broken." Their sister listened. "Then I shall not speak," she promised solemnly. "Please," urged the Ravens. "Please keep your word. The shirts hurt, the wings sting, the beaks shriek, the eyes cry."

And with that the Princess nodded and put her finger to her lips as a sign that she would not utter a word to a single soul for three years, three months, three weeks, and three days, until the wicked Witch's spell was broken.

And so the Princess made her home high in the hollow of an old dead tree and was silent while weeks and weeks went by. Then, one day, a young Prince, far from home and wandering in the forest, stumbled across a stream. He bent down into the flowing brook to quench his thirst, and as he cupped his hands in the sparkling water, a delicate handkerchief of finest lace swept past him. The Prince reached and caught it, then craned his head upstream to seek its owner. He could see no one from where he was and, curious, he set off following the sinuous course. Eventually, he came to a place where the stream widened into a small pond, and there, washing her clothes, was the Princess. The Prince called out to her, waving her handkerchief. At this the Princess, startled and confused, hurried away into the thick of the forest. The Prince pursued her until he came to the tree into which she had disappeared. He thought she must be a Spirit or a fairy or enchanted. Her bright eyes flashed at him, but she would not reply as he questioned her.

At length, settling on the ground beside her, he took out his food and offered it to her and she was famished and had some, and soon he set off talking again: of his past, his present, and his plans; and all the while he was thinking, What eyes! All the while he was thinking, To kiss that mouth! So taken was he that he quite forgot what he was saying and blushed and laughed and blushed, and the Princess smiled, her first smile in months, a smile that wrapped all the way around her heart and his heart and squeezed them tight together. And the handsome young Prince came back every day for a week and she practiced the smile until it was ready for him before he arrived, and soon he gave up speaking too and they were content simply to sit and hug on that smile. Until one day he could not contain his thoughts and said them all. "Love," he said, and "marriage" and "always" and "ever," and the Princess came away from the tree and they kissed and that was that. But the Princess, though captivated, though thrilled, though tingling, would not speak, not a whisper.

The Prince set her up on his horse and they rode the long ride to his

kingdom, and on the way he told her of his father, the King. And of his beloved mother who had died. And the Princess wanted to say "I know," she wanted to say "Mine too," but she could not, so she did not. And, at length, they were there at the gates of the palace, and — proud as you please — the Prince took the arm of his beloved and led her to meet his father and his new stepmother. King and Queen were on the balcony when the young couple arrived. The Prince embraced them, then fetched his shy sweetheart from where she lingered close by, nervous and unsure.

She could barely raise her eyes as he brought her to where they sat, smiling their greeting. The Princess curtsied shyly, then looked up and saw a kindly old King, white-bearded and twinkling. Her eyes traveled to the Queen. Her heart stopped. Her breath caught. There before her was her stepmother, the Witch. The Princess stumbled, fell to the ground, swooning.

When she came to, she was in a room of blue and beauty. The Prince sat by her, holding her hand. She told herself she'd had a nightmare, now she was dreaming. The King entered and smiled at her recovery. She'd been tired, he told her, overwhelmed. How touching, he said, how charming, and yes, she was every bit as delightful as his son had told him. The Princess fell back onto the feather pillows, relieved and relaxing for a second — yes, of course it was a nightmare! — but at that very instant the Witch appeared, carrying a tray of broth and bread and remedies, her entrance a sharp chill. The Princess could not speak, although her heart howled, but she could stare. No, she could not say, but she accused with her looks. "Killer of my father, bewitcher of my brothers," she accused, for she knew her father must be dead.

But for all her smiles of welcome, the Witch was as shocked as the Princess at their reunion. Here was a thorn come back to prick at her ambitions. And the Witch knew she must have done with her. Witch looked at Princess, Princess looked at Witch, and their purpose hardened. So the battle began. And all the while the Princess kept faith with her promise and did not speak, and every day was a day nearer to the time when she could say all that she knew.

The days went by and the Princess married the Prince. The moon was honey for them! Never were a couple more suited, more in love. Their hearts blossomed and were full and not a minute, it seemed, before a child was coming to bless them. All night the Prince lay with his head on his wife's round belly, a hand in her hand, listening to the child growing, kicking, wriggling. The spring came and there he was: a son! A boy! Eyes like jewels, a sweet precious bundle. And the young mother would have given anything, everything, to say his name, sing to him, whisper. But she couldn't, so she didn't.

Even the Witch seemed happy. She visited the young parents and their treasure, sweeping up the baby in her arms and billing and cooing. "He has his mother's eyes," cooed the Witch. "Lovely." Then she turned and smiled at her stepson. "Let's hope he has your voice, my dear." Then, returning the infant to its mother, she made to go, leaving the Princess with an ominous farewell.

"Look after him, won't you?" she said, all sweetness. "Hug him all up, little man."

And the Princess did, of course she did. She hugged him all up. All night he lay in her arms, a warm perfect parcel. Next morning, the Princess woke with her son still tight in her embrace, shawl wrapped round him, covering his head. She gently pulled it back to kiss his tiny cheek, but what she found instead was the cold white china of a doll's face, its lips grotesquely red, its painted black eyes staring at her. The Princess opened her mouth to scream, then bit back the noise and let out gasps, long silent howls that racked her poor body. Desperately she pulled on the bell rope by her bed, its violent clangs crying her anguish. The Prince came running to her, bursting into the room: "What? What is it?" Then he saw the doll unraveling from the shawl, the hollow fixed smile. "Where's the baby?" he asked, his heart thumping. "Darling, where is he? Where is our son?"

But the Princess didn't know, and couldn't speak, and their baby was nowhere to be found. The palace was scoured from top to bottom, day and night, the grounds searched, the forests combed. Nothing. No sign of the tiny child. And the pain of it, the pain, intolerable. The Princess could not be comforted, was inconsolable, simply sobbed silently, covering her head with the sheets. Until, one night, she slipped from her bed and went to the garden and, with her hands, dug a small hole in the ground and, bending to the earth, screamed with all her heart. Screamed and screamed her pain into the hole until morning. And it was better. And, looking up to the sky, she saw her brothers, the Ravens, circling above her.

While the Princess was in the garden, the Witch found the Prince sitting at the window, lost in his sorrow. She comforted him, massaging his shoulders. "Your father and I are so sad for you both," she sighed, kissing his head. The Prince nodded sadly. The Witch continued to rub his shoulders, her beesting smile ugly but unseen to the Prince. "Darling," she began, but then hesitated. "Yes?" asked the Prince. But the Witch seemed reluctant to continue. "What?" he insisted. "Please. Say what it is." The Witch shrugged, then went on. "You don't think—no, this is absurd; it couldn't be—you don't think the Princess didn't . . . want . . . the little baby, perhaps, and perhaps . . . No, impossible." The Prince was overcome with indignation. "She loved him!" he cried, wounded. "Of course she did," the Witch answered. "Stupid. Forget I said anything, please."

At that moment, the Princess returned, her cloak pulled about her, hood covering her wretchedness. The Prince went to her, drawing her to him, clutching her hands. "Dearest," he whispered as the Witch looked on. "Where have you been? I've looked everywhere." Then he noticed her hands, smudged with soil. He frowned. "What have you got on your hands?" he asked. "What's this? Is this earth?" The Princess said nothing, torn apart by her vow, bridling at the Witch's smirk. "Perhaps she's been digging a little hole," suggested the Witch. "No? Then what have you been digging?" she asked, raising

an eyebrow at the confused Prince. But the Princess would not reply, though she had so much to say. The Witch shared a quizzical look with the Prince, making of the silence a terrible confession. "It must pain you so much she is dumb," said the Queen carefully.

Two years and two months after the Princess took her vow of silence, another boy was born to her. And she would not let this precious son from her sight. Not for an instant. Night after night, while all slept, she watched over him and would not sleep, until one morning exhaustion overcame her and her eyes stopped fighting and closed, and the Princess sank into fitful dreams. When she woke, she feared the child stolen and clutched the tiny bundle to her, felt its warm wriggling. Relieved, she bent to kiss his sweet cheek, her own eyes barely open. Suddenly a shrill squeak sounded, and staring, incredulous, horrified, the Princess saw that in place of her son, a piglet, pink eyes glazed with fear, struggled from the shawl that bound it. Again the silent screams, the gasps, the frenzy, the despair. For neither could this second son be found.

And now whispers were whispered in the corridors of the palace. Two babies disappeared. "What kind of mother," the whispers asked, "who loses babies, who will not speak?" "Cursed," they said, these gossips. "Bewitched."

It was several weeks later that the Prince, confused, miserable, went to see his stepmother, high in her tower. As he entered her room, she slammed shut a huge book covered with strange signs and inscriptions. Dust flew from it. She smiled at him, unclipping her hair, which fell gray and white to her shoulders. Cats ran under her table, and other creatures the Prince could not have named had he seen them, which he hadn't. A pot steamed on the fire and gave off a sweet smell like incense, which made the Prince's eyes, still stinging from his tears, weep all over again.

He said nothing, but went to her, and they embraced, his tears, her soothing and syrup. The Prince stared ahead as he braced himself to confide his worst fears. "You know, before, when my first son—" He stopped. "You know you asked . . . and I said, I said impossible . . . but now, now I don't know and I'm frightened." The Witch nodded, holding him close, nodding, murmuring. "Now she is with child again," the Prince continued, "I could not bear . . ." His voice trailed away, tears consuming him. The Witch sighed her support. "Sh-h-h," she whispered. "I know. When the time comes, we must watch closely. We must love her very much but watch her closely. Don't worry. I'm here. Sh-h-h." She mothered him, wrapping him in her web.

The time came and the Princess gave birth to a third son, more exquisite still, delicate, perfect. The Prince was with her, and together they were torn between joy and terror as they gazed on their little miracle. In the palace, in the kingdom, celebrations were muted. No one dared risk a raised glass, a toast, a clap on the back. The whole world seemed to hold its breath. The Prince suggested to his wife that he should take his son away, somewhere secret, at least for a while. This echo of her father's solution and its fatal results served only to unsettle the Princess more, and she could not keep her hands from trembling. She shook her head violently, rejecting the Prince's suggestion, she lying in her bed, the baby in her arms, the Prince sitting beside her. At her refusal, the Prince stood up and walked to the door, and the Princess could just see the shadowy presence of the Witch standing in the doorway, could just pick out a few of the words that passed between her husband and his malevolent stepmother.

"I told you she wouldn't agree to it," she heard the Prince say. "Of course," said the Witch, smiling. "Well, stay beside her until the morning and watch close." Then the Witch walked confidently into the bedchamber and leaned over the bed. "Little lamb," she addressed the baby, "don't you worry. Your father will watch over you." As she picked up the baby to hold, the Princess snatched him away, clutching him for dear life. "Ah," sighed the Witch, frowning at the Prince. "Never mind." She left them there in the failing light, the flame from her torch dancing and guttering down the long passages to her tower.

And so the young couple sat, silent, their hearts full to bursting, each feeling alone, frightened, watching their tiny child, his fingers like stars. Both mother prayed and father prayed, crouched like sentries over the cradle. I will not sleep, they said to themselves; I will never close my eyes until this child is safe. And for hours they sat in grim resolve, lighting candle after candle, reciting their prayers, heads reeling . . . but the strain—the tiredness of the birth—washed over them, huge waves washing over them, lulling them to sleep, and for a minute, two minutes, three, they slept. And then the Prince woke.

At his side his wife lay, eyes closed. Her hair was gray; her face was gray. In her arms the shawl had unraveled. The Prince began to wail, an inhuman sound, which shocked the Princess awake. As she started, sitting bolt upright, the shawl fell away from her and ashes floated up from it, ashes everywhere, filling the room. "What have you done?" cried her husband in a voice that snapped from suspicion to hatred, his rage welling up in huge sobs. "What have you done with my children?" She could not answer him had she wanted, had she wished to break her promise, for her own voice was lost in her private nightmare. Tears ran through the gray dust on her face as the Prince, wild, tormented, railed at her for the murder of his sons.

The King charged in, the Witch at his heels, and there they all were, surrounding the paralyzed Princess, horrified at the scene. The Witch swept up the shawl and let the ashes slide from it. "Oh dear," she whispered in a voice heavy with shock. The Prince, maddened, spat out his accusation: "She's a Witch. You were right all along. She is a Witch." He covered his face with his hands. "My poor babies!" came his despairing cry. "My poor sons." His stepmother, the real Witch, nodded, sighed, spoke into her husband's ear. The King listened, choking his own hot rage. "Yes," he agreed. "Yes, she must be burned as a Witch." And the Witch, hardly able to suppress her triumph, glowing with it, added but a single word: "Tomorrow."

And so it was decreed that three years, three months, three weeks, and three days after she had taken her vow of silence, the poor innocent Princess would be burned at the stake as a Witch.

As they prepared the bonfire, she stared from her window at the sundial in the courtyard, still far from the midday when the fire was to be lit. And she hardly cared, with all that was lost: a father, a mother, her brothers, her babies, the love of a husband. She hardly cared for her own poor body. She was glad to be silent. She had nothing more to say to the cruel world. And at last they came for her and they took her to the place and they tied her to the stake. As the sundial neared the line of twelve, it was the Witch herself who lit the torch and carried it toward the bundles of hay and twigs, the flame aloft.

And then three Ravens flew above, wheeling and diving and crashing into the Witch, pecking at her eyes, screeching the while, "The wings sting, the shirts hurt, the beaks shriek, the eyes cry!" And she dropped the torch on herself, screaming as its fire enveloped her. In a second she was nothing but ashes and dust and fragments. A silence fell on the crowd as they looked on, aghast, as the Ravens circled. A silence so profound that nothing could be heard but the flapping of their wings in the sharp sunlight. Until a strange and sudden sound shocked the crowd from their trance. A voice was crying out, in release. A voice locked in, volcanic, suddenly erupting into the air: "My brothers! My brothers! My brothers!"

It was the Princess, free at last to speak and tell all. "My brothers! My brothers!" she cried, and with that the three Ravens fell from the sky, their wings dropping, feathers falling, and by the time they landed, they were birds no longer and there before the loyal sister Princess were her three brothers.

They ran to her and pulled her from the bonfire and hugged and kissed her, and now she could not speak for crying, and the Prince, her husband, came to her and wept with her, understanding nothing until the brothers pulled them both to a place nearby where three other brothers played: a boy, a toddler, and a tiny infant. For, of course, it was the Witch who had stolen the children away. She had cast them, newborn, down a deep, dark well. But the Ravens, who watched everything, had caught them up and cared for them and kept them safe for this very moment when they might be reunited with their parents. Oh, for every tear they had wept before, Prince and Princess now shed a thousand, clutching their children whom they had supposed lost, hearts full to breaking. They fell to their knees and praised Heaven. For all was restored. And good held sway. The girl who had kept faith and had but one face for everyone was rewarded with sons and brothers and a sweetheart and a crown. And she practiced her smile until it was perfect.

Now those of you who should know more
might question what has gone before.

Three minutes was the sand unused
when Princess shouted what she knew.
Well, for these grains of unspent time,
her youngest brother's wing remained.
He didn't mind, and nor do I,
So you, my dears, should not complain!

Hans
My
Hedgehog

MEN and women meet and marry and love, and from their joy children come. Kisses catch, hearts embrace, and all is happy: pearl after pearl until a necklace of happiness. Or so it can happen, so it is told in stories. But sometimes love can fill a house and still the house remains empty. The tears and laughter of children, the music of family — there is none of this. Silence casts a shadow on these childless couples and there are things they will not speak of, hopes that well up, then are choked back, because there is a space and nothing may fill it. Such a couple, good people, farm folk, lived a long time ago, far from where I sit, and for all their crops grew, for all their fine harvests, sorrow was their only child.

Imagine a warm night, a cold night, a night like this one or any one. Outside the wind singing its lament, inside the farmer and his wife sleeping, snuggled up for warmth. But when the farmer reaches out for his wife, he finds a foot where her head should be, and the murmur sighing from her is at his socks and not his ear. "Ho!" he starts up and calls to her. "Ho!" but she's not budging. She's there for a reason. "Just for tonight," she tells him. "It's worked for others, it might work for us." "Chucklehead!" muttered her husband. "Don't be daft. You're not going to get a child. You've gone past it and that's that. If you want company, have a widow up from the village. Now come up this end. I'm proper froze."

But the farmer's wife didn't want an old widow for company; she wanted a baby, a little thing of honey and softness, to wrap up in a bundle and sing to and snoodle with and hug to bits. She'd wanted this child for what seemed a lifetime until she couldn't bear to watch the lambing or the calves come or the eggs hatch, it hurt her so. She bought books of remedies, went to women at fairs, paid a fortune in charms, rocked out the long summer evenings and shivered the long winter nights, slept upside down in her bed, but still, still, still no baby came. In the stables, at the table, in the barn, she would harangue her husband with the hows and whats and whens of fertility.

They say if you stay three days in a snake pit . . .

They say if you bathe first in mud and then in blood and then in milk of nettle . . .

They say if you kiss a thrush, eat a worm, swallow a frog . . .

They say the embrace of a stoat, the dung of a weasel, powdered tassel of bull, spider's dew . . .

Any of these will get us a son.

The farmer could not listen. Off he would stomp to the fields. No one wanted a son more than he did. His bones went stiff in the wind and he couldn't bend as he once could bend. He chopped and scythed and bundled and milked and walked and cropped, and all the while he hoped for a little boy to sit on his shoulders, to push the hat down over his eyes and chase the sheep mad and worry the hens from their laying. Oh yes, he yearned. But he never liked to speak of it. After, he felt bad.

Nothing, however, would deter his wife. One night, she brought him a glass of brackish liquid. A wee tonic, she told him, to be drunk night and morning. His face darkened, wretched and frustrated, but she clung to him. "I want a child. I wouldn't care if it were a strange thing made of marzipan or porridge, if it were ugly as a hedgehog. I want a baby to wrap in a bundle and sing to and snoodle with and hug to bits."

Now to say you wouldn't care when you want something is a dangerous thing. That woman wanted a bairn so bad she wouldn't care what she got. If she got a hedgehog, she'd bring its snout to her breast. Ears twitched that shouldn't have listened. Even as she spoke, the room went chill with mischief and the trees slapped the windows, leaves flying off like words to those who shouldn't know of such vows. . . . No sooner said than done, she got her wish. No time at all, she has her boy, little ball as ugly as sin with a pointed nose and sprouting hair everywhere, a hedgehog baby with quills as soft as feathers.

You could not imagine a more curious sight than the farmer's wife taking this baby to her breast, a bundle of ticklish sweetness, perfect smile in a sea of silky quills, the brightest bluest eyes like afternoons in Arabia when there isn't a single cloud. No mother ever loved her babe more than this woman. She wrapped him in a soft warm shawl and sang him old lullabies and snoodled him and hugged him to bits. And she gave her little darling a name. Hans, she called him. Hans my hedgehog.

But the farmer could not look at Hans my hedgehog. He didn't see the eyes like sky, he only saw folk giggle. He didn't feel the softness, he only felt the pitying stares on him. He didn't hear the lullabies, only the gibes, the speculations, the tittle-tattle of small minds with much to murmur of. No, he wouldn't go out, would not be seen with the child, rage and humiliation boiling in him. And the farmer grew to hate his son, the hedgehog boy. Out in the fields he chopped and scythed and bundled and milked, and all the while the shame of what had befallen him turned a knot in his heart—one moment the rage swelling, the next tears, huge tears splashing his boots.

So the hedgehog boy grew up, day following day, week chasing week, and his coat grew thicker and his eyes grew bluer and his nose more pointy and he was the sweetest son to his mother; oh yes, he was a jewel at throat and wrist for her. Elsewhere the sneers and curses curled him up into a ball, the spite hurt his coat into spikes, the insults teased his quills into sharp protective needles. And if he came into a room, his father would leave it. If he crept up to touch his hand, his father would shudder. This was Hans's life, a world of light and dark. The farm, his home, full of animals who loved him, his mother's snoodling. The world full of folk who loathed him, his father's brooding. Village boys would creep up to the farmyard and taunt him with their village-boy taunts, their safety-in-numbers taunts, their anything-strange-is-ugly taunts, with their terrifying normalness, their ordinary apple-red faces, their shirt-out, slow-witted, thick-tongued taunts.

"Hey, beastie!" they would yell, smug as bugs. "Hey, hairy! Hey, critterchops! Hey, prickleback!" And Hans would curl up into his ball and shiver. Then they found a name that stuck, a name they scratched on walls, whispered when he could not see them, a name to haunt him. "Grovelhog!" they called him. "Grovelhog!" And Hans my hedgehog learned he was strange and he learned he was ugly and he learned to be sad and he learned the name that was given him. Grovelhog.

He retreated to the farmyard, to the animals. For every quill on his body, Hans had an animal for a friend, as many friends as he had quills. He had a special way with these creatures and they loved him. He could talk to them. If his mother was looking for him, she would always go first to the yard or the stables or the pens or the sties or to the place where the rooster strutted, a proud soldier of the hens. Hans tended to this bird, combed his comb, polished his beak, and fed and fattened him, and it wasn't long before the rooster was the biggest rooster you could imagine, a hugeness, a vast red rooster all plump and flush-feathered. Whenever the sadness came, whenever he caught his reflection in a pool, saw his strange boybeast face, Hans would run to these friends and be among them, for they found him neither odd nor strange but magnificent.

His father would come home from the fields and see the boy sitting amongst them, pigs nudging his cheeks, the cows caressing him, the dogs licking his hands, and he was disgusted. And if Hans spoke like a boy, he ate like an animal, snout dipped into the plate, lap-lap-lapping, slurp-slurp-slurping, unable to use a knife or fork. Until one day his father snatched the plate from his lips and cast it out into the yard, dragging his son by the ear, then driving him into the trough. "That's enough!" he cried. "Get out! Get out! From now on you'll eat outside with the other beasts!" And with that he returned to the kitchen and slammed the door shut on his son.

Darkness fell and the house was quite silent. Hans had not returned. In one chair the wife sat, her face caught by the firelight, the tears glistening. In the other was the farmer, thick brows knitted, face set, saying nothing, but sighing often, head bowed to the floor. At length, he stood up, took a coat and a lamp, and walked out into the thick black owl-hoot night. "Hans!" he called, swinging the lamp through the fields. "Hans!" he cried, picking his way through the woods. But his son did not answer. He lay all night among the animals in the wet grass, under the sky's black velvet, and he thought and thought until he thought a hole in the ground. He did not answer his father's cries, did not return to his mother's tears, just lay there silently counting the stars.

His father wandered the dark hours, a great needle in his heart, one moment the rage welling up in him, the next tears, huge tears splashing his boots as he tramped and tramped and called and called. Until, come the morning, wretched, the farmer returned, damp through and weary. There by the step, asleep, was his son, the Grovelhog, who had never once answered back or complained or ever been anything other than the best son a man could wish for. And the farmer wanted to pick up his boy in his arms and hug him and snoodle him and love him to bits. But he couldn't. He looked down at his pointy nose and his short arms and his quills and hair and he couldn't.

"I've trudged all night for you," he barked, kicking the sleeping child awake. "And now you'll not eat for a week off my food." Hans stood up, quills rippling up and down his back. "Father," he said in his flute voice, "I want you to do some things for me." The farmer was outraged. "You what?" he barked. "I want you to go to the village and have a saddle made for my rooster so I can ride him," Hans said. "And I want some sheep and some cattle and some pigs." Furious came the farmer's reply. "Oh, do you now! Fancy fine!" Hans nodded, undeterred. "I know which ones I'd like. And they would be happy to come with me."

"Come with you where?" demanded his father. "To where I go," replied his son. "Which is away. Which is to somewhere. Where I can't hurt no one and no one can hurt me." Tears and anger fought in

the farmer. "You can't go nowhere. What'll your mum say who dotes on you?" Hans did not reply but rubbed the tears from his blue blue eyes. Finally, he looked up and curled his mouth into a brave smile. "Father, all night I lay outside to understand why you don't love me. I've thought and thought until I've thought a hole in the ground. And now it's all right. When I have the saddle, I'll go."

And the farmer felt ashamed. He went to the saddleman and brought home a saddle for the rooster and he herded up the animals his son had asked for and he told his wife to pack a packed lunch, and all the while the Grovelhog sat on the stoop and waited until all was ready. Then he went to his mother and she hugged him and snoodled him and loved him to bits, then to his father, who wanted so much to but couldn't, and said goodbye and, before the farmer could stop him, hugged him with all his might, and his father knew for the first time how soft he was, all honey and sweetness.

Then he was away, the Grovelhog, flinging on the saddle and riding off, the strangest steed, the strangest rider, the strangest army of hens and sheep and pigs and cattle. His parents watched him until he was a faint smudge in the distance, the farmer stroking the quill he'd shed in goodbying, while his mother felt a crack faulting her heart, like a tiny pencil line. And with each hour the pencil line grew thicker and thicker until one day, not long after, her heart split in half and she died.

Twenty years later, a King got lost in a great forest. It was the kind of forest where the trees point down and the paths point in, and all you can be certain of is that you don't know where you are. And once the King was lost he got more lost, until he was well on his way to losing his mind. You could tell this by looking at him as he tugged away at his ear, which is a sure sign of that complaint. Oh yes, he was well on the way when he heard a sound that was a bitter sound and a sweet sound all at once, a music that began like hello and ended like goodbye. So, tugging his ear like billy-o, the King followed that sound through glade and thicket until he came at length to a clearing where animals roamed—sheep, cows, pigs, and hens. Huge, these creatures, and content, looking for all the world like what animals on holiday must look like. And behind them was a palace. A most extraordinary sight, a fabulous affair of glass and jewels and waterfalls. The King approached the great doors and knocked.

The tall creature who greeted him was neither man nor beast, but somewhere in between. He had the body of a warrior, the eyes of a Prince, but his nose was stretched into a snout, and sweeping back from his eyebrows to his calves bristled a battalion of gleaming spikes. He looked nothing less to the astonished King than half a man and half a hedgehog, which is precisely what he was.

The King sucked in his breath and introduced himself, telling of his plight and his pedigree, of his missing army and empty belly. The creature said nothing through all this, and the King, story told, looked nervously at the sharp spikes and waited . . . waited through a long and threatening silence. Finally, in a voice of dark woodwind, the creature spoke. "You are welcome, sir, in my house," he said, and bowed before leading him into a magnificent hall, where huge fires leapt and sparkled. There, already laid for two, was a table groaning with food. Straightaway they sat down and ate of the greenest greens and the sweetest sweets and the juiciest juices. And after, with the embers glowing in the fires and the sun drawing in, Hans my hedgehog, for so it was, took up his bagpipes and began to play. What songs these were! Haunting and sinuous, threading through the evening air. Laments that were bitter and sweet all at once, that began in hello and ended in goodbye. And before he could think I'm full now and found, the King was asleep.

How long the King slept, he did not know. Dreams came. Dreams in many colors that broke over him like waves, hugging his sleep, washing away his worries. He woke a new man, ready for anything, or so he felt, but my dears, what a sight greeted his bright eyes. For his pillow was transformed into a tree, his bed a mossy bank, and the view was not of the creature's Great Hall, which was surely where he had fallen into sleep. No, ahead of him, sparkling in the sun's kiss, was his own palace! How he had come there, he knew not. All he knew was joy, joy in waterfalls, joy cascading over him. And he began to dance as only Kings once lost and then found can dance. A jig. A jiggle-joggle and a leap. Then bagpipes took up his rhythm in a merry reel and, looking round, the King saw the hero of his hour, Hans my hedgehog, astride his giant rooster.

"Anything!" cried the King. "Anything you wish for is yours, for you have saved and salvaged me, you have led me from the labyrinth." But Hans would have no reward. He was ready to ride off. "I insist," insisted the King. "Name anything, dear friend." And a curious smile came to the creature's face, his blue blue eyes twinkling. "Very well," he said. "Then I ask for the first thing to greet you when you arrive in the palace, whatever that may be." The King thought on this request, imagining his first steps on reaching home. And he knew his first sight would be of faithful, flop-eared, worried-himself-sick-eared Wagger, the Royal dog. No mean gift, for this was a wonderful dog, long the King's boon companion. But the King agreed, nonetheless. His dog would have a merry life in the freedom of the forest, in a place where the animal was King. "It is yours," he told Hans. "The first thing to greet me." At this, Hans bowed in gratitude. "I'll collect my reward in a year and a day," he said, and without more ado turned the rooster and set off, a strut and a gallop into the distance.

The King watched him, hand held up in gratitude, then turned himself and hurried home, the delight of return engulfing him. Sure enough, he had no sooner set foot on the drawbridge than he heard a bark and a yelp of glee. Trumpets sounded a fanfare. The heavy doors of his palace swung open. And there before him, racing to embrace her long-lost father, was the Princess, his daughter.

He took her up in his arms, their tears blessing them as he swung her round and round and round. Then came Wagger, jumping up at them both, desperate for his master's attention. Bells sang out the King's return. Wonderful! they tolled. Hurrah! Hurrah! Then,

through this chorus of welcome, the King caught another sound on
the breeze, a sound both bitter and sweet, beginning in hello and
ending in goodbye. And looking up, still clutching his child, he
scanned the horizon. There on the very edge of the hills, he caught the
silhouette of his rescuer, pipes raised to the heavens. A chill panic
gripped the King. He dropped his startled daughter and let out a sob
of despair. It seemed to him as if a black cloud had fallen on him. For
in his excitement, in his delight, he had forgotten his promise and
now the weight of it crushed him. Not my dog, his heart cried
bleakly. Not my dog, but my daughter. My daughter . . .

A lot can happen in a year. The King settled into the dance of days.
The snow, when it came, covered everything. The sun stunned his
inner being. Only as the trees dried from green to russet and shed
their summer dresses did the King lie awake through the nights,
unable to sleep, listening as the leaves rustled, grazing the stone walls
of the palace. Fear took him fretting along the battlements, his eyes
squeezed to the distance, waiting, counting the days. And all the
while suitors from far and wide pilgrimaged to his kingdom, seeking
his daughter's hand. And all who saw her were beguiled. She was a
Princess of Sweetness and Cherry Pie. The King's nightmare, of her
delicate skin pierced and bleeding from the creature's terrible coat of
quills, haunted him until he wished he had never been found, longed
to be lost again in the forest. For he had spoken to no one of his rash
promise. To no one.

Oh yes, a lot can happen in a year; sometimes the minutes drift,
marooned, and a single afternoon can seem a lifetime. But when you
dread the future, days can make you dizzy with their dash. So it was
with the King. It was upon him, the fatal day, before he'd caught his
breath. A year had whizzed like a firework fizzing into the air. The
evening found him slumped glum on his throne. And when the bells
dully thumped out the hour at six, he was still there, gray and
dejected. At the last chime he heard another sound, a sound both
bitter and sweet, beginning in hello and ending in goodbye. And the

King stood up and moved stiffly to the balcony to observe the arrival of a strange creature, half-man, half-hedgehog, riding on a giant rooster and leading an army of animals. The King sighed and walked slowly down to the drawbridge to greet them.

"Do you remember me?" asked Hans my hedgehog, his voice half-pipe, half-drum. The King nodded. "A year and a day have passed since we last met," continued the creature, his coat of quills alert and dangerous. "Will you keep your promise to me?" The King's face set in a grim mask. "I will," he said. "I will."

Should I tell you of the Princess's tears, their torrents, her sighs, her lament? Should I tell you of the pain, how it hurt the King to say what had been unsaid, explain what was inexplicable? Let it suffice that for an hour, two, after Hans came to the palace, father and daughter were together alone in her chamber, and that when he finally emerged, the King could not raise his eyes but stared, bleak, at the ground beneath him. He led Hans my hedgehog to the chamber, then went himself—sorrow his crown, sadness his scepter—to his wife, the Queen, to tell all, to console and be consoled.

Hans found the Princess sitting at the window of her chamber, hair streaming down, coiling through the open shutters, as if her soul were contained in the auburn tresses and sought escape. He walked into the room and she jumped up. Jumped up before her betrothed. Her father had not exaggerated. She was promised to a monster. And yet, when the creature spoke, his voice was the voice she had always imagined her husband would possess, a voice of woodwind, of dark notes, a true voice.

"Do you know of me, Princess?" the voice asked. "I do, sir," she replied. "You saved my father and he owes you his life." Hans nodded. "But do you know of his promise to me?" he demanded. "He promised you the first thing to greet him on his return," she said, looking at the blue blue eyes, the pointy nose, the carpet of quills. "I am yours, sir, to do with what you will." The quills bristled, the blue eyes

sparked and flinted. "Then I claim you for my bride," he said. "I want you to come and live with me in the forest. I want you for my Princess of Sweetness and Cherry Pie. I want to catch you up and sing to you and snoodle you and hug you to bits. I want you to love me." A single tear crept down the Princess's sweet cheek. "Then so be it," she whispered. "Do you find me very ugly?" asked her husband-to-be. "Not so ugly as going back on a promise," she declared, and felt the tear slide from her face to the floor.

They were married the next day. A wedding without bells. A funeral of a wedding, the guests in mourning. No words passed between the couple save the "I do"s and the "I will"s. After, the banquet was presided over in silences punctuated only by the occasional sob—from Queen, from King, from Princess. Even the music threaded its way into the room as a grave and plangent rain. It followed the couple as they left the banquet hall and made their way to the bridal chamber, all eyes on them, a confetti of pity and outrage filling the room.

The fierce glow of the fire caught the highlights in the Princess's hair as she crept into bed. Red light danced around her face. She lay quietly in the lace and linen of the sheets. Her husband stood at the fireplace, staring into the flames, then picked up his pipes and began to play. The Princess closed her eyes and through the closed lids, saw her miserable future unfolding. Along the corridor in her parents' room, King and Queen lay listening to the pipes, breath held. Abruptly the music stopped. The Princess shivered. Next moment she forced her eyes open to see a grotesque paw, half-hand, half-claw, approach her cheek. His touch was so gentle, so careful. He brushed his hand tracing the perfect shape of her features. She shuddered and he withdrew his hand as if it were burning. His sigh left her as he retreated to the grate and lay down. And so, the air fragile with emotions, the bridegroom and his bride settled down to sleep on their wedding night.

What woke the Princess she could not say. A rustle, perhaps. Or perhaps the terror of her dreams, but when she opened her eyes she was astonished. For there, barely illuminated by the fire's farewell, was her Lord, the hedgehog man, peeling off his coat of quills, peeling away his hideous skin, to reveal the fine silhouette of a tall and splendid man, the quills settling like a rug on the ground. She watched, dumbfounded, as the man slipped quietly from the room and disappeared. And lying there, half-Sweetness, half-Cherry Pie, the Princess could hardly credit what she'd seen and couldn't have, saw and shouldn't have. But, creeping to the window, she looked down and there, sure enough, was a man, all shadows, moving among his friends, the animals, in the night's quiet rain. And she found herself going to the abandoned coat of hair and quills and touching it, soft and warm and remarkable.

The first rays of morning woke her from dreams of waterfalls and ice cream and there she was in her bed, and by the ashes and dust in the grate lay her husband, back again, beast again. So had she dreamed this peeling off of skin? Surely she must have. But that night, the same scene: the creature standing over her as she pretended to sleep, the tender touch on her cheek, not prickly but so smooth she felt an ache when he left her, and then the magic of his transformation, the emergence of man beneath the skin. And she wanted so much for this fair youth, slender in the shadows cast by the fire, wanted so much for him to come to her. But no, he slipped away. Again she crept to the window to watch him as he moved among the animals, as they nudged and nuzzled and caressed him. Again she went to the coat of quills and lay down against it, and how comfortable she found it, how luxuriant! It made her drowsy, lying there by the fire; it made her eyelids heavy. She sighed, wrapping herself in her husband's skin, drifting off, drifting off. She knew she shouldn't, knew she mustn't, but really couldn't help herself, really couldn't stay awake another minute.

A shadow fell across her face and its dark touch woke her with a start. Standing in the doorway was her husband. "Sir," she cried nervously. "I woke and you had gone! And left behind you your coat of quills." She could not see his features, his expression; he remained cloaked in the darkness. "Which would you have as husband?" came his reply. "The man or the creature?" The Princess thought on this, swallowed, considered. "I have a husband," she said, at length. "And he is what he is. No more. No less." She saw the stern shape relax, soften. "Then forgive him, madam, if he returns to his skin," said her husband as he stepped toward the quills and assumed them, restoring the beast's silhouette. "For I am enchanted," he continued, "and cannot leave it. But if you say nothing of this for one more night, then loyal love will break this spell forever." His blue eyes settled on her, yearning, imploring. Her heart reached out to him. "I promise," she whispered. "I promise."

But we all know about promises, don't we? And secrets. What use are they when no one knows about them? When they twist and turn and tickle our stomachs. When they are tickly little fish wriggling into our conversations. Now, you see, the Princess had a mother . . . and mothers have this way of catching secret-fish and promise-fish. They eye us with wise eyes and all our rivers are glass to them. They fish us. Just so with the Queen, who that morning at breakfast sees a daughter skip to the table, eat when for days no appetite, laugh when for days no laughter.

"Hungry?" she inquired, raising an eyebrow. "Very," replied her daughter, all Sweetness, all Cherry Pie. "Good," her mother said, smiling. "Sleep well?" The Princess ate heartily. "Yes, thank you." "Good," repeated her mother, eyebrow twitching, her voice casting its hook into the conversation. "Not troubled by the creature?" The Princess frowned. "No, Mother," she said, defensive. "And please don't speak of him as a creature." Her mother looked at her carefully, the hook dangling. "Listen, daughter," she began. "Last night your father and I went to a wise woman and told of your tragedy. She knows of these creatures, these Grovelhogs, and knows the remedy. He is enchanted, you see."

"I know," the Princess blurted out, the invisible hook snagging her

38

lips. Her mother pulled sharply on the line. "Oh?" The Princess felt her face flush flustered. "I mean, I knew he must be," she cried, wriggling away from the question. "Yes, I see," she pretended. "He's enchanted." The Queen reeled in, triumphant: "He's told you, hasn't he?" Her daughter denied it, all the while wriggling. "Does he take off his skin?" her mother demanded. "No!" she insisted. "No, he doesn't! He doesn't!" The Queen grasped her hand. "The only way to break the spell is to throw the skin into the fire. If he sleeps or leaves the room, cast the skin into the flames and he will be free of it." The Princess shook her head, confused, miserable. "That's not the way!" she cried, her betrayal exposed. The Queen settled back into her seat, the fish landed. "So he *has* told you!"

That night, the same story: the Princess settling to sleep, the creature stretched out by the fire. But when, at length, he stood and shed his skin and slipped from the room, the Princess rose from the sheets. Before she could stop herself, before the warring voices in her head could plead with her, she took up the skin and threw it into the fire's greedy flames. How it burned! A thousand colors, a brilliant firework! Suddenly, terribly, a cry of pain and rage curdled the air. There, below the window, stood her husband, the Grovelhog, beast again, smoke and flames consuming him, his head thrown up roaring out his betrayal, screaming his anguish. He threw himself to the ground smothering the flames, rolled over and over on the earth, while in the palace the Princess ran, ran along passage, ran down winding stair, until she was outside, running to him, tears scalding her, tears choking her. She reached him as he leapt up onto the rooster, as the animals stampeded for the gates. "Husband!" she wept. "Please! Please don't go!" But the creature snarled and turned away from her, his quills sharp and smoking. The Princess clutched at him and was pricked terribly, falling pierced and bleeding, while the Grovelhog rode off into the night in a confusion of smoke and dust, the air thick with clamor and alarm, the bells tolling their solemn knell: betrayal and betrayal and betrayal.

For seven days and seven nights the Princess of Sweetness and Cherry Pie locked herself in her room and would not come out, but stayed, prostrate on the wooden floor, sorrowing. And the days passed—sun, then moon, then sun—while she thought and thought a hole in the hearth until she knew what she must do. She went to the blacksmith and got from him three pairs of iron shoes, and that same night, while all slept, slipped out of the palace and set off to walk the world in search of her husband, half-man, half-hedgehog.

She walked and walked until she wore out the first pair of shoes, and still no one had set eyes on the creature. Such a walk she walked that her hair faded from red to brown. And she put on the second pair of shoes and began again, never stopping, always hoping. And the second pair of shoes wore out while her hair faded from brown to gray, but still she walked, always searching, always praying to hear a music both bitter and sweet, beginning in hello and ending in goodbye, but nothing, no clue, no news. Until one day, weary and wretched, she came to a stream and lay down by it. The last pair of shoes had worn away to nothing, and she pulled them from her, rubbing her poor sore feet, and saw in the water's mirror that her hair was now quite white. And the Princess of Sweetness and Cherry Pie wept for her red hair and her husband, both lost forever. Night was falling and the mist settling in, as it does in that season in that place, three pairs of iron shoes from anywhere. What could she do?

Then it seemed to the Princess that she lapsed into a dream. And in that dream she saw a bent figure walking the ground, his way lit by the swinging flare of a lamp. The man approached her, catching her face in the light, but instead of greeting her, he stumbled past, calling out into the mist. "Son!" he called, tears splashing his boots as he walked. "Hans!" The Princess got up and followed him, why she knew not, where she knew not, until they came to a cottage, an old farm cottage, long abandoned, swathed in cobwebs. Just as the cottage came into view, the lamp guttered, faded, and went out, and as the light disappeared so did the man. The Princess was at a loss.

What now? she wondered. She looked about her, shaking her head as if to throw off the dream, but stopped suddenly, for there sitting in the porch of the cottage, rocking on a rocking chair, a small bundle wrapped in a shawl tight in her arms, was an old woman. The Princess watched amazed as the woman pulled back the corners of the shawl to reveal a tiny creature, half-baby, half-hedgehog. She gasped and ran to the woman, but as she reached the porch the woman disappeared and the door swung open. In went the Princess, her heart in her mouth, but inside the house was empty, only dust on the table, dust on the shutters. She sank to the floor and fell into a deep, despairing sleep.

Something woke her. A flapping. A beating of wings. She was still in the house. She hadn't dreamed it. The morning sun was pouring in, sending the dust dancing in its light. The Princess crept into the parlor in time to see a great golden eagle fly in and land on a table, its huge wings folding into rest. The Princess shrank back from the bird. Suddenly it shook and trembled, and transformed before her eyes into a strange creature, the posture of a man, the skin of a hedgehog, quills quivering. The Grovelhog! Her husband! Fear gripped her. And trepidation. The Grovelhog sat at the table and food appeared, wine. He raised his glass, unseeing, while his wife looked on. "To the health of that most beautiful woman who could not keep her promise," he whispered, and drank down his wine.

The Princess stepped forward. "Husband," she said, taking her courage. The creature swung round, his voice filling with anger. "How did you find me?" he demanded, the quills spiking. "I have walked the world to find you," his wife replied. "I have worn out the soles of three pairs of iron shoes and my hair is no longer red. I come to claim you and catch you up and snoodle you and hug you to bits." And with that she flung herself at his mercy, risking the spikes of his rage. She clung to him as he struggled, clung to him as his body trembled into a transformation, wings unfolding and shuddering, clung to him as the shape of a man emerged, disappeared, reappeared, all the while

41

declaring her love and loyalty. She would not be thrown off, would not give in to the wings, to the spikes, to the violent shuddering, but held fast to her husband, until finally the shaking stopped and man and wife stood embracing, the spell broken. And they laughed and snoodled and hugged each other to bits, pain falling from them like feathers, like quills.

And so the Princess who could not keep her promise won back her husband through looking without hope of finding, and in time her hair grew red again and there was another wedding all over, and this time the feasting went on for forty days and forty nights and I myself was there to tell the best story there is to tell, a story that begins in hello and ends in goodbye, and for a gift they gave me a shoe worn to nothing.

And here it is.

The Soldier
and Death

Life protracted is protracted woe.
SAMUEL JOHNSON

HIS is the story of a Soldier, an honest soul walking back from twenty years of war, with nothing but a shilling in his pocket and three dry biscuits for the long trudge home. A thousand miles the Soldier marched and on the way had many an adventure, for he was a man of rare courage, oh yes, many a dragon, many a slip and scramble. And he spent his shilling and was down to the three dry biscuits when one day he came upon a Beggar playing a fiddle by the side of the road. And the Soldier, who, as ever, was whistling, a thin-between-the-teeth-type whistle, a long drizzle whistle that never remembered a tune, he stopped and joined in with the Beggar's fiddle; the one couldn't fiddle and the other couldn't whistle and quite happy they both were. And had he not stopped and whistled with that poor Beggar, the Soldier would never have begun the adventure that led to his tangle with Death himself.

For what could he give the Beggar for his merry reel but the first of his dry biscuits, for which the Beggar thanked him, wishing him a better whistle. Off the Soldier went with a light heart, and when he took up with his tuneless tune—well, funny peculiar and strange indeedy, he had a whistle like a . . . Well, imagine what rubies would sound like if they whistled, and you have it. Yes, that was his new sound, and he heard it and he liked it and he kept it up all the way down the road, until he met another old boy down on his luck and

43

worn at the edges, and this old man he played one he played knick-knack on his drum, and the Soldier stood and whistled his ruby whistle and did a little jig in his weary boots. But then he swapped a second biscuit, and now look at his dance! A fine terpsichore, good as new, a skip and a hop along the road, until at length he came to a third old soak, worn to a whisper and playing a game of solitaire by the road, and the Soldier looked as the fellow shuffled the pack and dealt out the cards, one after the other, a perfect hand. Now the Soldier had but a single biscuit in his bag and he was hungry as heck, so he thought on it. He pulled out the biscuit to break in two and share with the Beggar, but it didn't feel good, did it, to give the old boy less than the others, so he held out both halves.

"You're a good man, Your Honor," said the Beggar. "And deserve more luck than to be on your last biscuit. Take these cards, and may they never lose for you." And with that he held out the pack to the Soldier. Next he rummaged in his rags and fished out an old sack, which he held up to the Soldier. "And take this sack also, an ugly thing, but remarkable. Order a bird in or a beast or anything you like and it will be there in a twinkle." And the Soldier took it, thank you very much, and off he went a bright skip and a ruby whistle, a light heart and an empty sack, and walked a warm night and a bright day and came to a river.

Three fat geese swam here, their proud armada skimming the water. The Soldier took out his sack and loosened the cord at its neck. "Hoy! Geese!" he shouted. "Hoy! Get in my sack." And with this the geese flapped, scrambled, and flocked to the sack, one after the other. The Soldier was astounded. He was delighted. He swung his booty over his shoulder and headed for the town that beckoned on the horizon. How he whistled, how he danced. He had a magic sack!

That night he roomed in the tavern. The Innkeeper eyed him as he entered; the full sack, the Soldier's livery. "Home from the war, are you?" The Soldier nodded. "With a sack full of spoils." No, the Soldier explained. These were three geese, newly trapped. If the Innkeeper would cook him the fattest and give him a good bed, he could have the other two for his pains. This bargain was quickly struck, and after a time the Soldier settled down to a dish of goose roasted in clove and honey and a bottle of best liquor, and he ate it all and sucked the bones and drank the liquor and danced, drunk as you like, until the morning, when he sank, flopped, swam into bed.

Three days later, he woke up and looked out of the window. And there on the hill he saw a palace. Where once was pomp, now was ruin. Neglect had traced its moss and ivy, gouged out the stone. Menace issued from this place. The Soldier ambled downstairs and questioned the Inn-keeper. "That's the Czar's palace," the Innkeeper explained. "Was once a place of waltzes and chandeliers and fabulous parties. Now the Devils have it for their card games." The Soldier's ears pricked up. Devils? "Devils," confirmed his host. "Every night, they tumble in and scream and shout and play at cards. No decent folk go near, they are so devilish." The Soldier stepped out for a closer look. He asked the Innkeeper why no one had rid the palace of these Devils. His face clouded. "An army tried." he began. "In the morn-ing there was nothing left of them but shadows. I watched them, we all did, these shadows wandering through the great halls search-ing for their bodies, until the sun set and they faded away. A ter-rible thing. I tell you, these are devilish Devils and gamblers too." This was challenge enough for our valiant Soldier. Fetching up his sack and his wonderful whistle, he stalked purposefully toward the palace. The Innkeeper watched him march off and shook his head at the folly of it.

Inside the palace, the Soldier found dust, decay, and a devilish odor. A heavy silence settled around him as if the world were holding its breath. He sat in the banquet hall at a great table with its cloth of cobwebs, drummed his fingers, and waited for darkness to bring visitors. Hours passed. The shadows lengthened until only the gutter-ing flame of a single candle flicked on his face. He gazed at it. Suddenly clocks began a melancholy chime, creaking into life, and with them a scurry and a scamper. A rush of cold air extinguished the candle and all was black. The Devils had arrived. The Soldier felt them flapping like bats above his head. The doors to the hall burst open and slammed against their hinges. More Devils, hundreds of them, poured into the room, each carrying tiny torches. They swarmed to the table and surrounded the Soldier, who continued to sit, unabashed. He began to whistle.

"We have a visitor!" hissed one of the Devils. They were all identical. "He's whistling," said another. "That's a nice whistle. I want it." "Hello," said the Soldier, introducing himself. The Devils flapped above, around, and beneath him. They repeated his greeting to each other as if it were quite the most ridiculous word they had ever heard. "I hear you like a game of cards," the Soldier said. This produced an accordion of cackles. Each picked up this line and passed it to his fellow, then collapsed into a hideous hiss and wheeze, which the Soldier assumed was amusement. He smiled back and produced the Beggar's pack of cards, shuffling them and banging the stack sharply onto the table, causing dust to billow up and send the Devils into fits of choking. He dealt them out. "So," he said amiably. "What shall we play for?"

The Devils had ideas. His soul? His whistle? His teeth? The Soldier agreed. He would wager anything they fancied, soul, whistle, teeth, anything. But what would they offer? The Devils were crying with laughter at the idea of anyone imagining he might beat them at cards. The doors opened again, and minor imps appeared dragging forty barrels of gold and forty barrels of silver. "Any use?" inquired one of them as each of the players dipped into the gleaming coins and threw them onto the table.

The Soldier nodded, glancing at the money, then settled down to play. The cackling ceased as the Devils examined their cards. Cards were exchanged, legally and otherwise, then thrown triumphantly down. Each hand was better than the one before it. Piercing red eyes turned to the Soldier. He looked at the cards, then at each face in turn, before turning over his own perfect hand. "My round, I think," he announced, scooping up the coins. The Devils could not believe he'd won. Then the Soldier dealt a second time. And won again. Then a third. Gold piled up in front of him. Horns were shaken, wings flapped, tails slapped irritably from side to side. "Is he cheating?" said one to the other. "Well, *I* am and I'm still losing."

"Deal again," they told the Soldier. And he did, and he won. And the Devils got into the kind of fume only Devils can get in. He won game after game while the Devils cheated to high Heaven and low Hell to no avail. By the first bells of morning, the forty barrels of silver and the forty barrels of gold were stacked behind the chair of the Soldier, who whistled as he won.

"We'd better call it a day, my friends," announced the Devils' tormentor. "We will not," they fumed. "We will call it a breakfast and you the meal. Come, brothers, let's tear him to pieces!" The Soldier whipped out his sack and slapped it on the table. "First make sure who eats whom!" he cried and, opening the sack, ordered them in. With that, an invisible hand seemed to grasp them by foot and ankle, horn and wing, and squeeze them, one after the other, into the magic bag. Within seconds the room was empty save for the Soldier and his bulging, kicking, turbulent booty. Hoisting the sack over his shoulder, he marched into the courtyard and played merry hell with his captives, whirling them about his head before bringing them down to earth time and time again, with a bump and a bash and a thump and a crash. Fume! fume! fume! fumed the Devils in a queasy chorus.

"More?" demanded the Soldier. *"No, no, no!"* pleaded the Devils, shrieking in torment, swearing to make an end of their mischief. Whirling them around and around, their captor forced promise and vow from them. Never, they would never come back. Definite, they would cause no more harm. Yes, came their curdled oaths. Yes, yes, came their strangled pledges.

Satisfied, the Soldier untied the sack. How they swarmed from it, the terrified Devils; how fast they headed for Hell, wings beating madly. As they flew up and off, the Soldier grabbed the last of them, catching a despairing hoof, dangling the poor Devil above the ground. "Let me go!" it shrieked. "Let me go. I couldn't stand another blow." But the Soldier refused until the creature swore to serve him faithfully. "Yes!" yelled the frantic fellow. "I swear by toffee, swear by worms, swear by all those things which squirms, swear by murder, swear by boils, swear by muck and boiling oils." And so the Soldier released him, but kept his foot. The Devil crashed to the ground and stared, flabbergasted, back up at his little hoof in the Soldier's fist. "My foot's come off!" "That's right," agreed the Soldier. "Now off you go and remember where you left it."

Off he went, the little Devil, on his one good hoof, hop and howl, flap and foul, straight to Hell. Once inside, he and his fellows slammed shut the doors for fear of being followed by the Soldier and his sack. And they trembled and quivered and fumed and listened without speaking for three weeks in case they didn't hear our hero coming after them. But the Soldier had no time for Devils; he was the toast of the town and the star of the Czar. And things went well with him for a long time. He kept the Devil's foot. Black flowers grew from it, smelling of sulphur.

For a long time all was dandy for the Soldier and his sack. He took a wife, got a son. And lived with them in the palace that the Czar gave him. All good things came. Silks and satins and fine damask cloth. Sweet days. A hero's happiness. Our Soldier laughed long and whistled loud and was known to dance in all weathers. But fortune is fickle. He woke up one morning from his feather bed to find his son in a fever. For five long days and five long nights, he sat, the Soldier, at his son's side, wife beside him. But no matter the medicine, no matter the prayer, the fever raged and the sickness worsened. And so it was he lost his whistle, and so it was he lost his jig. And his wife shed bitter tears as the child faded from them, tossing and turning in his torment.

And they called for quacks and apothecaries and healers and men with needles, leeches, quicksilver, and long words in Latin, and soon the boy's room was full of graybeards and shaking of heads, but still the fever raged and the boy passed into a swoon. The graybeards were replaced by priests mumbling and praying and rattling their rosaries.

And a man in black came with a vile stick to measure a coffin. The Soldier and his wife stood and watched and sorrowed, chill shadows lengthening across the room, their son's face growing paler with each hour. "What shall we do?" cried the Soldier's wife. "My lips are sore from praying and my knees weary of kneeling." The Soldier shook his head, hopeless, full of anguish. "It's the very devil," he sighed. "The very devil."

Now that's a word. Devil. It went out of his mouth and straight into his ear and jiggle-joggled his memory. And as it did so, the foot, forgotten in the corner, began to shake, its black flowers quivering. The Soldier saw it and yelled out, "Now where the devil's that Devil of mine?" No sooner said, no sooner done, than a flash of smoke produced the Devil, his sworn servant, bowing and at the Soldier's service. "Where've you sprung from?" inquired the Soldier. The Devil shrugged and pointed wryly at the thin angular stalks of his legs. "Not so much sprung as hopped, Excellency. You have my foot." With this the foot shook even more. At once, the Soldier proposed a bargain with the Devil. If he could cure his son, the Soldier would return the foot.

The Devil considered for a moment, then produced a small, beautiful glass, a tumbler of jewel and crystal, full of water. He held the glass up by the sick boy's head and peered into it, squinting at something, nodding the while. Satisfied, he hopped to the Soldier and beckoned him to do the same. The Soldier took the glass and looked through the liquid at his son. Standing at the foot of the bed was a strange figure, a dark hood shrouding his face, so that the Soldier could not tell whether he was young or old, this creature. Indeed, the face seemed to the Soldier to be that of an ancient baby. All that was clear to him, through the glass and crystal, were the eyes. Black. Extraordinary. Black like a night in the wilderness. To look into them was to look at the darkest sky. Thick black with stars.

"Such eyes!" the Soldier exclaimed. The Devil beamed. "That's Death, Excellency. But do not fear. See how he stands at the foot of the bed." The Soldier nodded, entranced. "All is well," explained the Devil. "If Death stands at your son's feet, he will recover. Only when he comes to the head must you worry. Now, splash some of the water from the glass onto your child."

So the Soldier dipped his fingers into the glass and let the drops fall onto his son's head. At once, his son shuddered and opened his eyes. He looked up at his father and mother as if it were a morning like any other and he had just waked. "I'm hungry," he said, and sat up.

"Oh heavens!" cried the Soldier's wife. The Devil coughed. "Oh Devil!" she said to appease him. And what a marvel it was, their son as good as new. They danced, they sang, they whistled. "Could I have my foot back?" the Devil inquired hopefully. The Soldier promised he could have back not only foot but freedom in exchange for the marvelous, miraculous glass. And the deal was done with joy on both sides, the Devil hopping

off clutching his foot with its bouquet of black flowers, the Soldier nursing the magic glass, his wife their darling son.

So it was that our friend the Soldier set up in the time-honored trade of miracle man, and soon all the graybeards and all the prayermen were out of business as he traveled the world on a camel with his magic glass. Show him a sick man and he would hold up the glass. If black-eyed Death sat at the foot of the bed, a quick splish-splash and up the invalid would sit pouring out blessings. If Death stood staring up the other end, the Soldier would shake his head solemnly and depart: "What a pity I came too late," and so on. And the relatives would mutter, "What a pity he came too late," and pay him all the same. But as often as not he left with all happy and amazed and praising him. And it went well for the Soldier until one day, far from anywhere, he gets a message from home to say the Old Czar has fallen ill and sends for him.

So off he set, from the far off where he was, riding all night, riding all day, until home and hurrying to the palace—doors flung open, fifty of the Czar's wives weeping in the long corridors—and into the bedchamber where his patron lay, gray and giving up the ghost. All hoped and all prayed as the Soldier took out the glass and held it to his eyes. But what the Soldier saw was Death smiling by the Czar's head, waiting patiently to carry him off. The Soldier frowned a frown and he sighed a sigh. "I've come too late," he said, and shook his head. One to the other the wives carried the news, a sob passed tear to tear down the long passages. "He's come too late," they wept. "He's come too late." And they complained to the Soldier, saying, "You save beggars and thieves and cats and dogs and yet you cannot save your master." But if Death wanted a new friend, the Soldier knew he could not fight him. So he thought on it and thought on it and knew what he must do. Once again he held up the glass, and for the first time he addressed the black-eyed creature. "Sir," he said. "The Czar has been my friend and father. Take me, and spare him, I beg you."

The black eyes stared back, unblinking. A hush settled on the chamber. Silently, Death came down from the head of the bed and stood, eyes fixed on the Soldier. Swallowing back his fear, the brave man dipped his fingers in the glass and blessed the Czar, who sat up in an instant, praising Heaven. And while the palace cheered, bells ringing, the Soldier slowly turned and left, a sad and solitary man trudging home to meet his end.

By nightfall, he had taken to his bed, the life flowing from him. His dear wife and son sat by him, helpless. It seemed all up with him. His energy ebbed away, his breath was shallow, his heart was weak. A frail arm held up the glass, and the Soldier dimly saw the black eyes watching over him. With a final effort, he reached under the blankets and heaved out the old sack, waggling it under Death's nose. "Do you know what this is?" he asked of Death. And Death replied, "A sack." "Well, if it's a sack," exclaimed the Soldier, "then get in it!" Suddenly the sack bulged as if gulping in the air. A suck, a hiss, and a whoosh. Quick as a flash, the Soldier leapt up and yanked the drawstring tight. Then he was jumping up and down on the bed, his family looking on in amazement. "I've done it!" he cried triumphantly. "I have captured Death in my sack!" And he had. Imagine the dancing, imagine the whistling, imagine the hugs and kissing! For the Soldier had done the impossible: he had cheated Death. He laughed the laugh of a man who could not believe his fortune. He threw the sack in the air. Death his prisoner!

The news, whispered from one of the Czar's fifty wives to the next, spread through the town as fast as gossip, which is what it was, and nothing spreads faster. Within four and a half minutes the whole town knew and within seventeen minutes the whole country knew and by the following morning it was the news in a thousand languages. Death a prisoner! *Morte un prigioniero! Tod ein Gefanger! Smird ooznitzen! Ekhmalotisame ton thanato!*

And the Soldier, to be on the safe side, set off with Death in his sack

and found the thickest forest and the highest tree and clambered up it
and hung Death from the longest branch, and promptly fell off. But
there's nothing like Death off-duty to cushion a fall. For now, of
course, nothing could die. Relatives gathered at deathbeds for months
on end. Crossed lovers would throw themselves off cliffs and have a
long climb back. Everywhere the oddest battles ensued! There were
wars going on in most places and they became very strange. At the
end of a day's carnage, flashing swords and explosions, the air thick
with arrows and the savage swoosh of axes, nobody had died! The
armies would look at each other, exhausted and intact. Duels at dawn
went on till midnight when the rivals would go home confused. And
our friend the Soldier was the most famous man in the world. Because
suddenly everyone could live forever. He sat in his palace and whistled
his ruby whistle.

Then one day, looking down from his window, he saw his gardens
full of poor souls wandering, old scrags of folk barely held together,
a frail funereal march. The Soldier went down to them, approaching an ancient lady, a gray-and-white cloud of a woman, so fragile it
seemed any moment a breeze might lift her from the ground and
blow her away. When the Soldier asked of her purpose, she replied
in a reedy voice, in a voice of wind chimes, explaining that they
were all of one will. They were waiting to die, they had given
up the ghost.

"Ninety winters I'd seen come and go," she whispered. "I was but
an hour away from peace when you tied up sweet Death in your sack."
And what was true for her was true for them all. They were weary of
age and its sucking out of spirit. "Long ago our place in Heaven was
made ready for us," she told him sorrowfully. "But for you, we would
no longer drag our misery about the world. Let us rest in peace." The
Soldier looked about him and saw a sea of faces implore him, for these
old folk were not afraid of Death, only of the long dying. And they
were not alone. Thousands blew out their candle that night, hoping it

55

was their last, but a new morning betrayed them. These deathless ones pilgrimaged to the Soldier's house and stood with the others under his window: a swelling, wailing, groaning crew, until the Soldier could not bear their limbo another minute.

Once more he set out for the thickest forest, found the highest tree, climbed it to the longest branch, and there, hanging, was his sack. He sat on the grass and untied the drawstrings holding in Death. As he picked at the knots, the Soldier spoke, declaring his surrender. "I've led you a merry dance," he admitted. "Now you must have me, and set the world to rights." But no sooner had he loosened the ties that secured it than gusts of what seemed like air billowed from the sack. Death was fleeing from him. "Come back!" the Soldier beseeched. "Death! Come back!"

But Death had fear of him and his sack, and would not come back. Again, the Soldier was condemned to watch while others aged and died, but Death would not come for him. He lived on and on until he could stand it no longer, and dragged his dust and fragments across to the edge of the Earth and slowly down to Hell, where he found a huge door that had no top, no bottom, and no sides.

The old Soldier went up to the door and gave it a sharp knock. From every conceivable place, a smaller door opened, and from each popped the head of a Devil. Smoke wisped out behind them and ghastly groans. The heads swiveled and looked down on their visitor. "A sinful soul comes to surrender his life," announced the Soldier. And just about to let him in were they when one of them noticed his luggage. "What's that you're carrying?" it asked suspiciously. The Soldier shrugged. "A sack," he said. Every door slammed shut. For the Devils remembered that sack and would have none of it. Where could he go? wondered the Soldier dismally. Where could he go with the burden of his sins weighing heavy on his old shoulders? An idea came to him. He hammered once more on the grim door and hollered at the Devils. "I won't go," he told them, "unless you give me the map to Heaven and a way in." There was a silence. Then a map landed at his feet. Encouraged, he continued: "And two hundred souls you have no use for." This request prompted a hiss of whispers and furious discussions from behind the massive portal. Doors were opened, then shut, steam belching from them. Then a Devil stuck out his crimson head and waggled his horns at the Soldier. "One hundred and fifty," he bartered. The Soldier brandished his trusty sack. "Do you know what this is?" The Devil shrank from it, crying, "Don't wave that sack around!"

Suddenly the door swung open, creaking and complaining. Fug and foul issued forth, a dense bilge of sulphur and reek. From this unholy smoking stench, two hundred slow and mournful figures emerged, heads bowed. The Soldier examined the map as his sorry charges, lifeless and vacant, awaited his instructions. The parchment was a mess of hieroglyphs and strange signs. "Follow the directions," advised a scrawl scratched on the back, "until you can go no further. Then go directly up until you have the sensation of standing on your head. This is the edge of Heaven. Thereafter follow the church music." Thus informed, the Soldier turned and set off, while the Devils peered through cracks and crannies and fumed.

The ragtag pilgrimage made its way through thick cloud and thin cloud, through twist and turn. Some time later (how long he could not tell, for they had long since passed the place where there is night and day), the Soldier had the strange sensation of walking upside down. He paused, halting the procession. And listened. From above him, organs sounded, and celestes and the flutes and oboes of Paradise. Guided by his ear, they continued upward, always upward, the music swelling, their spirits soaring, until there they were at Heaven's Gate, so bright they could not see it, so dazzling their hearts beat fast. A voice greeted them. A voice like bells, like nothing they had heard before, an Angel's voice.

"Who approaches?" asked this perfect voice, and the Soldier stepped forward bravely. "I am the Soldier who took Death prisoner," he told the light, "and I have brought two hundred souls from Hell in the hope that God will forgive me and let me in with them." Without hesitation the Angel replied, "The souls may enter, but alone." The Soldier felt the clouds fall on his head. He turned to the souls. "Go then," he told them, "and be blessed," then stood, heart heavy, as they passed him, one by one, the last few steps to peace, the last few seconds before an eternity of rest. The Soldier twisted the sack round and round his hand while he felt hope drain from him, happiness slip away.

Then, just as the last few were running, stumbling, running to the always and thereafter, a thought, a brilliant thought, came to him and he reached out and touched the shoulder of one of the pilgrims. The Soldier slipped the sack into the soul's hand and whispered to him, "Take this, friend, and once inside, call me into the sack. Remember: I delivered you from the furnace." The soul nodded, smiled, and moved on. The Soldier watched him as he disappeared into the blinding light.

The Soldier waited and waited, an inch from Paradise, waited for what seemed a lifetime. But, you see, there is no memory in Heaven. Nor guile. Souls forget. The Soldier stood in vain. For howsoever life may smile on us, the laugh is reserved for Death. After a long time the Soldier, abandoned, went slowly back to Earth. And for all I know he wanders still, as we all do, between Heaven and Hell. But if sometimes, just before sleep, or at places where sand meets sea, land meets sky, you hear a sound like the sound of rubies whistling, you can be sure it is the Soldier and that he can still jig. I know, for he himself told me this story and afterward we danced until dawn.

The
Luck Child

NOT so long ago, here in the deep north—
where it can be so cold just very cold is
considered quite warm—two dark hearts
ruled the land. One beat cold in a cruel King
and the other in a terrible beast, a Griffin. And
it happened in a week with two Fridays that the
cruel King heard of a prophecy. A child had been born,
reported his spies, a Luck Child, poor as penance,
rich as snow, the seventh son of a seventh son. Wise
Men prophesied this child would one day be King and claim all the
riches of the realm. "Superstition, Majesty, folklore," advised his
evil Chancellor. "Old wives' tales. How could a peasant's child,
not worth a spit—how could a brat become King?"

But the cruel King choked on the news, could not swallow it, felt it
sharpen and pierce his heart. So he vowed a cold vow the boy would
not live to see the snow melt and the summer come. And before dawn
he set out with his Chancellor to find this Luck Child and do him in.

Now the boy they sought was indeed a humble child. Even as they
rode, King and Chancellor, through the bleak hills and barren lands
of the realm, even as they planned their wicked wiles, a tiny infant was
at his mother's breast, rags to swaddle him, huddled for warmth, poor
as penance, rich as snow. Gifts came for him, scraps of food, thin
shawls, a blanket, for folk in these parts knew of the blessing of a
seventh son to a seventh son and honored it. And joy warmed the

simple hut where his mother lay and his father watched and his brothers slept. The Luck Child's sweet smile echoed in the room from mother to father, from brother to brother. And they lacked nothing except the full belly and the wherewithal to fill it. While baby fed and family slept, the father went from boy to boy, collecting strips of clothing, ripping his own coat, to make do for his new son, and he thought the while on the long winter and how he might feed them all. May the days bless us, he prayed silently, and the nights protect us, and the Lord watch over us. "Amen," whispered his wife.

A harsh knocking broke the silence. The father went to the door and opened it to the weather. Standing there he saw two men, hooded against the wind, fur framing their faces.

"We come in search of the Luck Child," said one of them sternly, peering in at the cradle. "Is this him?"

The father said it was indeed so that in those parts they counted such a child as lucky, although they had nothing in the way of fortune for him. One of the men dipped into his cloak and produced a purse. From it he took a thick gold piece and held it up for them to see. The last flickers of the fire caught the gold and it sparkled. Husband and wife had never seen gold and were startled by it. Neither spoke. The man shook his purse, which jingled. "My master here, a good man, brings seven pieces like this," he declared, the gold jingling in evidence. "He seeks a child to patron and to care for." At this, the second man stepped forward, face in shadows, and nodded. "As if he were my own son," he said quietly. The first stranger explained their mission. They would swap the seven gold pieces for the Luck Child. He and his master stood, impatient, while husband looked to his wife and then both looked sadly to the floor. "It's a bargain, I take it?" asked the first man. "Yes or no?" cajoled his master.

Finally, the mother spoke in a small voice. "He's my little boy," she said, not looking at the strangers and their bag of gold, but pleadingly at her husband. The first man dismissed this with a wave of his hand. "You have six others, Mother," he said curtly, "and now they'll be plump as pigs." The mother wept. The children woke. Her baby began to cry. "He's my little lover," she whispered, and held the tiny bundle to her. The first man sighed. "Well, of course," he said in a sour voice, "you must have more gold to comfort yourself," and dug into his pockets for a second purse. "'Tis not more gold my missus wants," said her husband, standing by her and placing a protective hand on her shoulder. "You can't put gold to your breast. You can't hear its heart beat."

At this, the strangers dropped their guise of generosity. The evil Chancellor, for it was he, addressed the father in his real voice, a poisonous hiss. "Please yourselves," he hissed. "You've had your chance." And so saying, he turned to his master, the cruel King. "I'll send in men on the morrow," he told him, "and turn the snow bloody."

And the father heard these terrible words and had fear for his family, who one by one had waked and clung to him and to each other, threatened by the two hooded strangers. He looked at his wife, hugging the precious baby. They could say nothing, but their hearts spoke. What could they do but sacrifice the one for the sake of the others? What could they hope but that these tall men with their rich furs and bags of gold would take the child and care for him, hoarding his luck? The father bent down to his wife, and gently unclasped her hands from her baby, kissed his tiny forehead, and gave him to the Chancellor. "We'll hand over our little boy to your safekeeping," he said sadly. The Chancellor snatched the baby away, tossed the purse into the empty cradle, and headed for the door. "Look after him, eh?" cried the father. "Because he's a little precious, you see. The seventh son of the seventh son." His voice cracked with emotion. "He's a Luck Child." The two men, hurrying out, left no words of comfort behind them. The door, flung open in their wake, chilled the room.

And that was that. Husband looked at wife, who looked at children . . . one, two, three, four, five, six. No one spoke for a long time. In the silence the cradle swung, jingling the gold pieces. Had it been filled to the brim with gold, it could not have comforted them.

Outside, the two men rode on through the bitter cold while the snow pinched and punched and slapped at their faces. On they went, their grim hearts set, until they came at length to where black cliffs traced the edge of the kingdom, a dreadful drop from land to sea. They left their horses and hastened to the brink, the Chancellor carrying the Luck Child in his arms. And after looking down to watch the waves crash against the rocks below, the Chancellor turned to the King, shouting to be heard. "The fall will finish him, or the icy waves!" Oblivious to this terrible scheme, the Luck Child smiled, a charming smile that touched even the King's hard heart. "That's a nice smile," he said in a troubled voice. "I'd smile, too," returned the Chancellor, reminding him of the prophecy, "given your kingdom, given your gold, given all that is rightfully yours." "Would you?" the King asked sharply. The Chancellor caught his suspicion and was at pains to explain. "I wouldn't, sire," he insisted, scrape and grovel. "I mean *he* would! I speak of him!"

The King nodded, eyes narrowing. "I can't look," he said, pointing to the drop. "How far down is it?" The Chancellor bent over the edge to estimate. As he did so, the King placed a boot on his back and kicked him over the brink, sending him flying into space, dropping, dropping like a stone, the baby with him, hurtling into the black jaws, the infant's shawl unwinding as they fell, a white flag unfurling in the darkness. "That's right!" cried the King. "You go too, sir! No one will share my crown!" And he shook his fists at the air in triumph, his own roar merging with the Chancellor's as he crashed to the ground, the rocks and waves rushing up to meet him.

And the cruel King turned and went back to his horse, his heart pounding at the deed, the baby done for, the prophecy denied. But had the King looked, had the King watched, the sneer would have left his lips. For the baby fell, oh yes, he plummeted down, dropping into the dark, the sea roaring below, the black rocks beckoning—oh yes, he plunged downward. But remember: this was a Luck Child. The shawl caught on a jutting rock and wound round, pulling the baby up short before dropping him gently down onto the shore. Sand, soft, safe. The evil Chancellor fared less well. The sea had him. As for the cold King, the days went by, and from time to time he thought of the Luck Child, and felt a little bad, a tiny bad, a fleeting bad . . . but soon he quite forgot what he'd done out of fear of a prophecy. Besides, it wasn't long before he had a baby of his own. A little girl. She sought out the one soft part of his heart and touched it. How he loved his little darling! And the years passed, ten, twelve, fifteen, sixteen; the daughter turned out a beauty, a lovely. A princess talked of. Longed for. And the offers! Hundreds. But the King was vexed. He didn't want her married. He wasn't going to lose her in a hurry, or his money, or his jewels, or his castles, or his crowns, or the things he wouldn't even mention in case anyone stole them. Hands off! is what the King thought. Hands off all my lovelies!

Greed grew in him like a canker until he could enjoy nothing, until he would not count his gold for fear of rubbing it away with his fingers. Instead, he traveled his kingdom, inspecting harvests, collecting taxes, worrying each farthing into the Royal Coffers. And always the King wanted more.

So it was that one day he came to a mill busy with the reckoning of the crop. All morning the men had come, trundling in the carts loaded with their year's efforts, knowing that for every sack they might keep, the King would take two. Inside, the Miller ground the grain while his son wrote the figures in a ledger. And though much was given away, enough was kept, for the sun and the rain had come that year in plenty and the harvest was good. So spirits were high, and the Miller's wife went among the men with a cup of cider and a heel of bread, and who didn't sing clapped, and who didn't clap laughed, and all was merry.

Then trumpets sounded as the King approached, and the mill fell silent. In he swept, glaring at the gathered sacks, noting the big pile that was his and begrudging the small piles that were not. All bowed and cowered at his entrance, save for the Miller's son, a handsome youth with golden hair, who remained at his seat as the King strode toward him.

"I am in your region inspecting harvests," announced the King. "How goes it?" The Miller's son smiled. "Fair, sire," he said pleasantly, and handed over the ledger. The King checked each entry with a sour eye, his finger running down the list. "Am I cheated?" he demanded suspiciously. "I will not be cheated." The boy shook his head. "No, sire," he told the King, and then continued in a bold voice, for he was a brave fellow: "I have counted each tithe and entered it. Your people sweat for each ear of wheat, each cob of corn." The Miller chimed in anxiously. "And Your Majesty also needs his tithes, of course." "Of course!" agreed his wife, their eyes darting to the King to see if this appeased him. The King glowered at them. "That's right," he said threateningly. But the Miller's son was undaunted.

"That's right," he echoed, smiling the while. "Otherwise we'd all be Lords and no King, and then what?" All around the mill, the peasants, still kneeling, shrank back at this daring and waited for the King's response.

The King walked over to the Miller. A shadow crept across his brain, nagging, nagging. "How come the boy is fair?" he asked suspiciously, "when you two are dark?" The Miller coughed nervously, glancing at his wife. Before he had time to reply, his son answered for him. "I'm a foundling, sire," he said easily. The shadow over the King deepened. He stared at the boy, his eyes fixed on the smile, wondering why he felt he'd seen that smile a thousand times before, in his dreams, in his waking thoughts. "Found where?" he demanded. "Found when?" The Miller placed a protective arm around his son. "By the black cliffs," he mumbled, his voice faltering. "Seventeen years since. Washed up without a scrap on his little body." The King's heart began to race. "You're a lucky one, then," he said. Father and mother nodded, relieved. "That's what we call him!" said the Miller enthusiastically. "Lucky!"

Now the King knew the worst, knew where the shadow had come from, knew why the smile had haunted him. Bile curdled his mouth, and he gasped, hardly able to catch his breath for his thumping heart. For he knew the boy must be the one born to claim his throne. The Luck Child! Kill him! thumped his heart. Kill him! Kill him! Kill him!

Biting on his lip, the King stared at Lucky. "A boy like you would do well at court." he said. Lucky's face fell. "I am needed here, sire." "Then you'll be missed," snorted the King, turning to the parents. "I'll take the boy." With that and brooking no disagreement, he took pen and paper and began to write. "Take this to the Queen," he instructed Lucky. "It's a Royal Warrant. She'll welcome you into our care." After sealing the paper, he handed it to Lucky and left, as he had left once before, stealing a child from its parents. His Page stepped forward. "Hurrah for the King!" he cried, a sharp look

66

requiring agreement. "Hurrah for the King!" the peasants chorused. "Hurrah for the King!"

So that night the Luck Child, after seventeen years of peace and happiness, set off alone on his Royal Errand, oblivious to his own true identity, oblivious to the King's foul designs, oblivious to all save the sorrow in his heart, the sad farewells to his mother and father, the past behind him, the adventure ahead. He clutched the Royal Warrant and pushed on. But there was many a mile between mill and palace. Many a forest. And Lucky had no horse or map. The night settled on his head like a huge cloth, and he was very soon lost. He went round in circles, hungry and tired, missing the harvest dance and the cider and the pretty village girls. Head fuddled, he plunged once more into the trees. But a man on foot could not fathom this place. Folk went in, but few came out. And foul things lived there. Owls hooted, branches rustled, the wind moaned, things slid and slithered underfoot. Lucky shivered, pressing on, full of courage. Until suddenly, without warning, the ground gave way beneath him and before he knew it he was falling for the second time in his short life . . . down and down and down . . .

Lucky was in a hole that sucked him up, pulling him into its stomach. He dropped for what seemed like minutes and then crashed, smashed, and dashed on the bottom. Dazed and bewildered, Lucky opened his eyes to a strange sight. He was in a cave, an inch from a bubbling cauldron, and all around him as he peered into the dim light, he saw treasures and trophies piled on the ground. A voice from nowhere made him jump in surprise. "Oh dear, oh dear, oh dear," it said. Lucky turned, searching for the speaker, but saw nothing. "Oh dear, oh dear," the voice repeated, and Lucky looked down and saw the smallest man he had ever set eyes on, a tiny, bearded, shifty chap, with darting eyes and a little skipping shuffle. "Oh dear, oh dear," he continued regretfully. "You've fallen in among thieves. This is a Robbers' cave. A terrible place."

Lucky explained he was on Royal business, and showed the Little

Man his letter from the King. The Little Man shook his head and looked anxiously about him. "I see," he muttered. "Oh dear. Are you hungry?" Lucky looked about him, searching for an exit, but there didn't seem to be one, save the endless hole from whence he had come. He turned to the Little Man too late to catch him add a dash of white powder to the bowl of steaming stew he had dished out. "It's goulash," announced the Little Man, handing him the bowl, producing an old bent spoon, which he huffed and polished on his filthy apron. The stew smelled delicious, piping hot. "Thanks," said Lucky, accepting it with relish. "I'm supposed to be Lucky. That's my name . . . Lucky. But I don't seem very—" And that was as far as he got, for a single spoonful of the Little Man's goulash sent him reeling to the floor in a stupor, spoon and bowl scattering with a clatter.

"That's it!" the Little Man shrieked, hovering over Lucky's drugged body. "I'm the cook, also the poisoner, also the nastiest!" And with that he set about searching the boy for booty. But he was disappointed. Lucky had nothing, not a sausage—only his Royal Warrant, poking from his pocket. With a tut and a cluck and an irritated hiss, the Little Man snatched up the letter and broke the seal with his knife. "A letter from the King, eh?" he muttered. "Well, this will never reach the palace. Oh, no—your luck's run out. Oh dear me, yes." So muttering, he sat on a rock and began to read.

The Little Man could not believe his eyes. Terrible! What a terrible letter! "This is terrible!" he announced. And this is what the letter said. "Wife," it began, "when you read this letter order the bearer of it, a youth named Lucky, to be chopped into a thousand pieces. Do this without delay. King." The Little Man was outraged. "This is disgusting!" he declared, and regarded Lucky with pity. "Poor fellow," he said, all heart and sympathy. "We'll soon see about this!"

Now he was also a forger, this Little Man. Full of fair play, he sat down to write a new letter. Oh yes, he sat with his wax and his quill and a ready will and practiced the King's sly script until even the cold

Monarch himself could have seen no difference. And then he began to write. . . .

So it was the next morning, and the Luck Child woke refreshed and restored and—remarkably!—with the palace straight ahead of him. Very odd, he thought, but off he set without more ado, blessing his luck and brandishing his letter with the Royal Seal. He didn't see the Little Man watching from the woods, a benign smile on his little lips, a gleeful twinkle in his little eyes. Lucky blessed his luck and hurried on, hole, cave, and goulash fading from his mind as he viewed the finery before him. "I have a letter from His Majesty!" he cried, at the drawbridge, "A letter from His Majesty!" at the entrance to the court. In he went to find the Queen sitting stitching at the open window, and in a chair beside her, weaving at a loom—with eyes like licorice, smile like Heaven, hair like silk, and skin like satin—was the Princess, her daughter.

And a thing happened straight off: Lucky looked at the Princess, the Princess looked at Lucky, and that was it. Love! Oh yes, as the perplexed Queen greeted this unlikely youth and opened her husband's letter, Lucky quite forgot where he was or who he was or why he was there, and dropped into the deep for a third time, dropped into the licorice lakes. The Queen, meanwhile, read and reread the letter in her hand, her glasses falling from her nose. "Gracious!" she cried. "Well, gracious me!"

A week later, the King was on his journey home. A boo to him and a hiss. He gloated. He gloated on the gold, on the riches squeezed from the poor. Each tiny speck of something—a brooch, an earring, a wedding ring, gifts from husbands to wives, mothers to daughters—plucked from the ears and fingers of his people, dropped into sacks to bloat his coffers. But it was not the wealth he was dragging home that drew the sneer across his evil face. No, it was relish. He was savoring his cruel deed, savoring the Luck Child in bits. He rode along contemplating the boy in a thousand pieces. How many pieces to a hand, he wondered? To an ear?

A mile from the palace he heard bells. A party of bells. A delirium of bells. He could not hear for bells. He called for his men to investigate, but they could not hear him for bells. And at the edge of the palace, hundreds of people cheering, or so he guessed; he could not hear the cheers for bells ringing, but their happiness was clear in the sea of flags, waving, dancing. . . . And then, looking up to the battlements, the King saw something and he couldn't believe it. . . .

For framed on the Royal Balcony, waving down to the crowd, the Queen smiling behind them, stood the Princess and Lucky, both in white and lace, hand in hand, strewn with confetti.

A noise came out of the King's mouth. A howl. A cry of rage, rage, rage. His heart thumped, his veins popped out of his neck, his face went puce, then purple, then thunderously dark. "*Oh!*" he howled. "*Ohhhhh!*" His daughter, his future, his precious treasure, standing there embracing the Luck Child for all to see. "How? How? How?" he howled. But no one listened.

"How?" he demanded of the Queen as he burst into the court. His wife hurried toward him, equally bewildered. "You ordered it!" she cried. "On pain of death." The King thought his heart would shatter. "I ordered him to be chopped into a thousand pieces!" He read the letter the Queen thrust at him. There it was, in his own hand, the Luck Child must marry the Princess. "Marriage on pain of death," ordered his handwriting. "Do this without delay, King." The King's head sagged, the letter slipped from his grasp and floated to the floor. His head filled up with the words of the prophecy, repeating over and over like a spell. "The Luck Child will one day be King. The Luck Child will one day be King." He couldn't shut out the words from his mind. "The Luck Child will one day be King. . . ."

The Princess saw her father and rushed in from the balcony. "Father!" she cried, leaping into his arms. "We're so happy!" And following on, looking every inch the Prince, came her husband, the Luck Child. "Majesty," he began humbly, kneeling in front of the King. "Forgive me. I had thought you a cruel tyrant, a blight on the poor. But now you make this humble peasant your son and heir and the happiest husband there ever was." The cold King couldn't look at him. He turned away, his brain grasping and clutching. Then it came to him. The solution. The only solution. A thin smile creased his mouth, his eyes glinted. "And the Golden Feather?" he asked innocently.

Lucky was confused. "Beg pardon?" "The Golden Feather from the Griffin," the King said impatiently. "Do you not have it?" The Princess looked at her mother in horror. "No, sire," said Lucky. "Then you must fetch it," the King told him, his smile thickening into a sneer. "Was it not understood my daughter could not marry without it?" "But that's impossible!" cried the Princess, clinging to her husband. "The Griffin is a monster. It eats people! It's terrible!" "She's right," said the Queen sadly. Oh yes, she's right, thought the King. I have him now. Now I have him. "Yes," he agreed aloud. "It won't be easy. But then not every man is fit to marry my daughter. That is the condition. The Griffin's Golden Feather."

"Very well," said Lucky with a deep breath, and though the Princess wept, though the Queen sorrowed, though the King smirked, he strode boldly to the door. "Don't worry," he told them, gathering up his courage, "I'll come back." But the Princess wept and wept. "No one has ever come back," she wept. "We'll see," said her husband defiantly, and without more ado set off in search of the Golden Feather from the tail of the Griffin.

Off he marched, the Luck Child, his chin a determined jut. To the Griffin, he told himself. To the Griffin. It became a direction when he had none, a distance when he knew none. "What do you seek?" folk asked him. "The Griffin." "How far do you travel?" "To the Griffin." And he paid no heed to the warnings, the weeping at his folly. No, he marched on. With each month his resolve strengthened. With each mile the land got poorer. Green gave way to dust. On! No lush, no life. The black deserts of the Griffin. On and on he trudged, until one day he came to a lake where no fish swam, and in the middle of the lake was an island and in the middle of the island was the shattered lair of the Griffin.

Lucky looked and was dazzled. For the island was pitted with jewels, the shore dusted with gold. It sparkled, cold as flint, on the black mirrors of the water, and a fine mist rose around it and crept to the far bank where Lucky stood wondering how he might cross. Soon he could see nothing at all, the mist enveloping him. A curlew called and then Lucky heard a bell, a handbell chiming sorrowfully across the water, sounding nearer and nearer, bringing with it the dim shape of a boat, a small craft steered by a tall stooping figure.

"Hey, Ferryman!" called Lucky. "Will you take me across?" The boat slid into the shore and there before him was the oldest man Lucky had ever seen. His white hair and white beard engulfed him, leaving only the eyes, dark and haunted, and the mouth, pale and wan. "I go across, back and forth ceaselessly, with you or without you," said the Ferryman in a voice of funerals. And Lucky barely had time to step onto the boat before the old man did indeed push away from the bank and set off slowly into the mist.

"I seek the Griffin," Lucky told him, holding on to the sides of the narrow craft, the Ferryman poling sadly through the waveless water. The Ferryman simply nodded and said nothing. Lucky peered into the mist, the world silent save for the curlew calling and the steady rise and fall of the oar. The island loomed before them, the jewels shimmering. "Such jewels!" sighed Lucky. "Such riches." "No one brings them back," replied the Ferryman, his own voice shrouded in gloom, his head bowed wearily. "I shall," announced the boy, determined. "I shall come back." The Ferryman shook his white head, the eyes hollow. "Ah," he murmured. "If you do, perhaps you'll discover why I must continue this weary way, back and forth, without ending. For I am tired and sick to my soul." And so saying, the Ferryman reached the opposite bank and Lucky leapt off the boat, all youth and courage. "I'll remember," he promised, and turned to wave, but already the craft had set off again, sliding into the mist, the Ferryman's bowed head slowly vanishing.

For each one who came, the same tale: the Griffin, please, for love, for justice, for fame, for fortune . . . but always in the end for the Griffin's supper. The Ferryman turned and pushed down his oar away from the bank, not wanting to hear the boy's cries, the splintering bones, the suck-suck-suck of juices.

Lucky walked into the Griffin's ruined domain. The great beast had ripped open the roof, smashing through the stone and timbers, turning what had once been a palace into a vast filthy nest, lined with muck and bones and things spat out. A dark, dank, damp stench overwhelmed Lucky as he wandered the hall, the stone flagstones bare save for a table large enough to seat a hundred men, but with only a single, massive chair set against it. Lucky shivered as the cold air whistled through the rafters, and he looked up at the black night and the moon above his head. Evil hung over him like foul breath, and for the first time in his brave life he knew what fear was.

A scampering noise startled him and he jumped round, dagger at the ready. "Oh dear, oh dear," said a familiar voice. Lucky couldn't believe it! Looking up at him was the ragtag and darting-eyed Little Man. Lucky was relieved and delighted and said so at once, embracing the Little Man and wondering what on earth he was doing there. And the Little Man told him that the Griffin had smashed open the cave and carried him away. His cooking had saved him, he explained, and now he was a servant for the terrible monster. And then Lucky said he'd come for the Golden Feather. The Little Man's face fell. Impossible, he told Lucky, impossible. But Lucky had come too far to hear these words again. He'd made a solemn promise to his wife. By hook or crook, fair means or foul, he had to have the feather. The Little Man scratched his little ragged head and sent clouds of lice buzzing angrily about him. "Hide under the table," he told the boy. "And I'll do what I can." Lucky hugged him with glee and made for the table, crouched under it, then popped his head out. "I must also discover how the poor Ferryman can cease his ceaseless crossing."

Before the Little Man could reply, a huge shadow threw the hall into darkness and high above them they heard a dreadful beating of wings. "Quick! Quick!" urged the Little Man, and Lucky dived back under the table. As the furious beating grew louder, the Little Man scampered to the kitchen, where an enormous pot of goulash simmered, and added the entire contents of his sleeping herbs, enough to send an army to sleep. Then, with a terrifying thump on the floor of the hall, causing dust and bones to jump and shudder, the Griffin arrived.

The beast that filled the banquet hall struck fear in folk's hearts and haunted their dreams. Misbehaving children were threatened with his name, the sight of him flying through the clouds sent strong men screaming for safety. The Griffin was immense. His massive head, half-lion, half-dragon, sat on the body of a giant golden eagle. His claws could rip a tree from its roots, his wings could slap down a house. He was neither good nor bad, not knowing the meaning of the words. He was simply hungry, always hungry, and when he was hungry, his rage was horrible. . . .

Lucky could only see the Griffin's talons. They had landed by him, crushing an abandoned skull into dust. He shrank into the shadows of the table and waited. The Griffin threw back his head, his huge nostrils heaving like bellows. "My sniff snuff snaff manwhiff," he complained, snorting. The Little Man appeared, dragging the steaming pot of goulash. "Of course you can smell a man," he cried cheerily. "That's me!"

The Griffin shook his head, his wings restless. "No," he said dangerously. "Snuffle snort other sort." Lucky tried to make himself invisible while the Little Man fussed and soothed the Griffin, clucking and cooing and stirring the pot. At the sight of the food, the Griffin's beak unclamped and a cavern of a mouth appeared, a mouth big enough to eat a house. "My could eat a house," said the Griffin, and with that he dipped his beak into the goulash and within seconds the cauldron was licked clean, goulash and sleeping herbs sucked into the bottomless stomach.

The Little Man watched carefully, but the potion seemed to have had no effect on the monster. He belched, a gust of goulash smothering his cook, and then demanded a scratch, as was his custom. "Scritch, itch, scrutch, scratch!" he demanded, and the Little Man clambered up onto his back to oblige. The Griffin loved to be scratched. He twisted and turned and arched and purred while the Little Man ran his nails through the feathers. "Yum, mmmm, eummm, ohyum," he sighed, delirious. The Little Man preened away, working his way up toward the single Golden Feather on his back. He tugged at it.

"Eeeeeeeech!" roared the Griffin and reared up, his wings suddenly flapping with a horrible violence. The Little Man clung on for dear life. "I know!" he cried desperately. "Clumsy, I'm clumsy, I scratched too hard." "Yowch," sulked the Griffin. But he would not let the Little Man stop. "No!" he ordered. "Itch scratch scritch." And so the Little Man did, obediently working at the feathers until he felt the monster relax. Once again he took the Golden Feather in his hand and pulled on it. "Yeowch!" cried the Griffin, and before he could avoid it the Little Man found his face sandwiched within the Griffin's beak, a gulp away from joining the goulash. "I'm sorry, I'm sorry," he moaned, his head as fragile as an egg. "Oh dear, oh dear."

"My not like things pulled," said the Griffin. The Little Man tried to nod his head but couldn't. "No, that's right," he agreed. "You're a sensitive monster." The Griffin was briefly pacified. "Yas," he said, then thought on it. "Not monster," he corrected. "Beastie" tried the Little Man. The Griffin shook his beak in disgust, opening his wings to crush the Little Man against the table with a single claw. In the commotion, the Little Man managed to grasp and hang on to the Golden Feather, so that as the Griffin reared up it came away in his hand. He dropped it as he lay prostrate on the table, the Griffin's claw pinning him casually, talons three inches into the wood. In a flash, Lucky shot out an arm, gathered up the feather, and retreated back under the table. "My bird!" insisted the Griffin, oblivious to all this. "My misunderstood bird. My not beastie!"

The Little Man could hardly breathe. "Of course you are," he wheezed. "A bird. A very nice bird. I should go. I should go back to where I came from. To that dark, horrid cave. Serve me right." "No!" roared the Griffin, prodding him. The Little Man gasped for air, the claw all but smothering him. "Don't try and stop me," he gasped. "I'll tell that old Ferryman to row me across. Yes, he's outside now, I expect, waiting for a passenger." He gasped again. "I'll go. Poor fellow, why's he always there? Why can't he leave?" The Griffin threw back his head dismissively. "Is curseddeworst and staydesame less someone take pole then someone cursedesameways him, so on so on so on," he clucked. "Simple."

Underneath the table, Lucky, clutching the Golden Feather, listened hard to this, but understood nothing. "So if someone took the pole from him," asked the Little Man, more familiar with the Griffin's curious expressions, "they'd have to row and he'd be free? So simple. I should go and tell the poor fellow. I should take over. Really. I should go now and take over." As he said this, wriggling to escape the Griffin's suffocating claw, the misunderstood bird relaxed his grip while a massive yawn overcame him. "No!" he exclaimed, yawning. His claw slipped away from the table, and his wings stretched in tiredness. "Go to sleep now," said the Little Man, scampering free. "Busy day ahead. Eating people and wreaking havoc."

The Griffin laughed and yawned all at once, the sleeping draught muddling his thoughts. "Ya zzzzz now then," he said wearily. The Little Man stroked the Griffin's beak as it slumped on the table, eyelids drooping. "That's it," he said. "Snoozie woozie." And in a second the lids dropped shut and the Griffin was asleep, his head rolling over and crushing the Little Man again, his nostrils puffing in and out peacefully.

At the first sound of the Griffin's steady snore, Lucky crept out from under the table, brandishing the Golden Feather, beaming with delight. The Little Man whispered to him to be very very quiet, and then, as Lucky stole forward to help disentangle him from the snoozing Griffin, he shook his little head, patted the Griffin affectionately, and told Lucky to go, Godspeed, take care, stay lucky. And so he did, leaving the huge Griffin and the Little Man, unlikely companions in the fading evening.

Off the Luck Child scurried, clutching the Golden Feather, scooping up jewels, scooping up gold; straight home he wanted to go, straight home to happiness. He waited impatiently at the bank for the sorrowful bell of the Ferryman. As he poled slowly forward through the mist, the old man could hardly credit what he saw, but there he was, the smiling youth, leaping onto the boat as it turned and headed to the opposite shore. "I dare not think it possible you have the answer," he asked, his white head shaking. "But then you did come back. No one has ever come back." "Well, I have come back," said Lucky triumphantly, "and I do have the answer." And this is what he told him. "The next passenger you have, hand him your oar. Then your luck will be his, his freedom yours." The Ferryman's eyes misted over. "By handing him the oar?" Lucky nodded, beaming. "That's it," he confirmed. "Simple."

The old Ferryman was moved to tears. "So simple," he sobbed, remembering a thousand crossings, a thousand thousand crossings, an age of crossings. "So simple," he said, and the tears ran from him. And for the first time in years, centuries, hope fired the Ferryman. Because—for all the tears—a smile was forming in his mind, a tiny smile growing, getting ready to be born.

The King was in his Counting House, smelling his money, when a trumpet sounded a fanfare. A great cheer went up on the ramparts and battlements. The King was paralyzed. The cheering grew louder, the bells started up again, and as he forced himself to the window he knew what he would see below. His Page burst into the room. "He's come back!" he cried. The cold King's heart thumped and thumped. In rushed the Queen, her face alight. "He's come back!" His head throbbed. In came the Princess, and before she could speak, her husband, the Luck Child, appeared brandishing his trophy. "I've come back!" he cried. "And I've got the Golden Feather!" He had done as bidden and the King could do nothing but agree and give his blessing. "You have my blessing," he said, though it cost him dear in his bitter heart. Then Lucky, his smile torturing the King, pulled open a chest loaded with the treasure from the Griffin's island. The King whimpered, his eyes popping, while the boy, his arm embracing his darling wife, explained his adventure. "I took a ferry across a lake to where the Griffin lives. On the other shore, gold lies where pebbles should, emeralds where sand. And where the sea breaks, diamonds fall."

The treasure burned into the King's eyes, the want welling in him until he was giddy. "Lucky," he mumbled, swallowing, swaying, skin turning hot and cold. "So lucky." But even as he spoke, the poison swilling his eyes, souring his mouth, the King vowed to go himself to the black lake. Greed will be my guide, he told himself; gold my map. That very night he slipped away alone, leaving his daughter and the Luck Child to their joy, and set off in search of the magic shore across the lake. And, at length, he found the lake and took a ride with an old white-haired Ferryman who seemed to row ceaselessly back and forth, tolling a sad bell while the curlew called in the mist. And he wanted the boat to go faster, faster, faster, and the Ferryman offered him the fatal oar, telling him there was, indeed, a way. . . .

So if you come one day to a black lake where the curlew calls and there is an island in the mist and a ferry goes back and forth, back and forth, rowed by an old sad man, turn around: Griffins live there, you may never get off the boat. For the Ferryman was once a wicked King who ignored a prophecy. And nature, my dears, is a wise woman who pays us back, tit for tat.

The
True Bride

TROLLS come at the bottom of the list of
people you'd want as friends. They can't even stand
each other. The Troll in this story had a daughter and she left home straight off. In her place the
Troll found an orphan, a young girl named Anya,
to wait on him hand and foot. But this girl had
more in store than to do for a Troll, oh yes; she had a
destiny. . . .

Now whatever the Troll asked of her, Anya did. She never
stopped, dawn to dusk, would clean and dust, polish and
scrub. She had neither father nor mother and the Troll was the
other, so she gave him her duty, cruel though he was. But one thing
the Troll could not stand was virtue. He did not like charity or
hope or kindness or generosity—any sort of virtue you can think
of he was against. So for every delicious meal, darned shirt, gleaming floor, there would be a terrible price. A slap for the meal, a
kick for the shirt, a spit for the floor. Yet woe betide Anya if these
things were not done. I should have said Trolls are always contradict-
ing themselves. And the Troll liked to contradict himself with a
heavy stick he kept hung on the wall. It made a horrid sound as it
flew through the air onto Anya's back. Blue, it contradicted on her
back. Black and blue. The harder the poor child worked, the harder
the tasks the Troll set for her.

The Troll was so ugly he would have no mirror. He could not stand
his own smell. He moved like a huge rat, scurrying along, his tiny

legs overbalanced by a head the size of a boulder. He had fat where there should have been muscle, muscle where there should have been fat, and bones in all the wrong places. He slept standing up and ate lying down. Hair grew from top to bottom and up his nose, and his teeth didn't fit in his mouth. His words came out in a jumble, his jumble came in out words. What he chewed he should have swallowed, what he swallowed he should have chewed, and his stomach had a hole in it. He was full of contradictions. He looked at Anya and found her too willing, too nice, too sugar and spice, too much what he wanted. So he resolved to ruin her.

One morning, he trotted in with a bundle of sacks and dumped them on the floor where

Anya was sleeping. "I'm off without," he announced, his head in the wrong direction. "Inside these sacks are being twenty pounds of feathers. Clean them and pack them before I come back," he instructed and disappeared. Anya rubbed her eyes and stared bleakly at the mound of sacks. Just as she untied the first of them, the Troll's huge head swung round the door. "And remember," he remembered, "I'm being allergic to feathers. A single one floating in the room upsets my nose a-quivering and a-quaking, a-rocking and a-rolling, a-shimmying and a-shaking. And I don't like it! So woe betide me if I be sneezed. Am I clarified?" And thus confused, he shot off again.

Alone with the sacks of feathers, Anya threw up her hands in despair. How could she, before the day ended, finish such a job, how could she? Soon he'd be back, the terrible Troll, soon his stick would contradict. So, trembling, wretched, she began to work. She plucked and cleaned and packed and packed, but still the feathers filled the room, still the feathers fought the sacks. After an hour, the room was full of feathers floating, feathers everywhere. Brave though she was, and not a little stubborn, poor Anya's heart sank. Is there no one in the whole wide world, she thought, to take pity on me? The clock chimed and shook her from her misery. Sniffing up a tear, she went back to the swirling feathers.

Then she imagined that someone had called her name. And the voice she heard was rich and warm and hugged her, and spoke her name in a way that made the word seem different, for she had no father nor mother, and when people said "Anya" it was always barked, hissed, yelled, or shouted. This Anya was a nice sound, and she looked round to see where it had come from. Standing in front of her was a Lion. A great white Lion with a mane like snow. She gasped and fell back, terrified. The Lion pad-padded toward her until his head seemed to fill the room. But when he spoke again, his voice was so soothing that all Anya's fears ebbed away. "Don't be frightened," he told her. "I've come to help you." "Where have you come from?" she asked. And the Lion explained that he'd come from her thoughts. "Is there no one in the whole wide world to take pity on me, you thought. Well, there is." And with that he asked of her task and told her to sleep, sleep, and dream it done. Anya meant to say she couldn't sleep, meant to speak of the Troll's threat, the terrible stick, but before she knew it, she had lain down on the flagstones, her eyelids so heavy, her dreams racing up to meet her; before she knew it, her eyes were closed and she was in a deep slumber.

An hour later, the clock chimed and she woke, startled, full of anxiety. The first thing she saw was the Contradiction Stick, cold on the wall. She must work, she must get busy. But when she looked, when she noticed, when she took in the room . . . what a sight, what a wonder! For there before her were the sacks, neatly bound, the work done, not a single feather forgotten. "Oh thank you, Lion!" she cried. "Thank you!" but the Lion had gone, and in his place was the sound of scurrying she knew so well. The Troll was returning. . . .

"I've recurred," he announced as his head appeared, then his body, then his legs. He licked his horrid lips and skipped over to the wall to collect his stick, relishing the swoosh and thwack. Only then did he see the sacks. "You've done it!" he gasped, his mouth dropping.

"You've done it!" Anya nodded, hardly believing it herself. "I'm gast and flabbered," muttered the Troll. "I'm founded dumb!" He poked suspiciously at the sacks, untying one. As he did so, his nose began to quiver, his nostrils dancing. A tiny feather escaped from the sack. "Aaaaachoooo!" he sneezed, and a cloud of feathers flew up in his face. "Aaaaachoooo! Aaaaachoooo! Aaaaachoooo!"

The next morning, the Troll woke Anya before the birds had begun or the light had appeared. "Arise and wakey!" he growled, shaking her. "I'm having another job for you." And while Anya struggled to open her eyes, he set about locking a chain to her ankle, meantime licking the two teeth that protruded from his lower lip. He dragged the sleepy girl from the house, yanking on the chain so that she could barely keep her balance, but must hop and jump behind him, the clasp biting into her flesh. "Come on, come on!" the Troll roared. "Haven't got all daylight," and he pulled her to a pond at the back of his garden.

"Observe this pond," said the Troll, observing it. "Deep, you'd say, and you'd be right. Depth aplenty." He pulled out a ladle from his pocket and thrust it into her hand. "Drain it," he ordered, his little legs rocking under the weight of his head. "Drain it with this ladle." Anya looked at the ladle, then at the deep pond. "If I be returning back and forth and find a single drop of water, if I so much as gets my foots wet"—the Troll stabbed one of his three fingers at her menacingly—"then heaven help me!" With that, he tied Anya's chain to a tree and skipped off with a cruel giggle.

Alone, Anya bent to the pond and dipped in the ladle. As she retrieved it, the water poured through a hundred tiny holes . . . for the Troll had given her a sieve for the task. Impossible! Impossible! She tried and tried and cried and cried until her tears raised the level of the pond more quickly than the sieved ladle could reduce it. She slumped back on the bank in despair, rubbing her eyes with her fingers. When she opened them, she was face to face with the great

white Lion. "Oh, Lion!" she cried. "My ladle is full of holes, my tears increase the water."

"You're tired, my little," whispered the Lion. "Lie down and sleep a while." Anya shook her head. "I dare not," she told him, "for my Lord the Troll will beat me with his terrible stick." But even as she spoke, she felt so drowsy, so heavy, so pillow and blanket, that she lay back in the grass and in a moment was asleep. And in her dream the Lion pad-padded to the pond and drank and drank and drank his fill until he had drunk it dry.

When she woke, Anya saw a hole where once there had been water and she could not believe it. "Oh, Lion!" she cried, but again he had disappeared. And in due course the Troll returned. . . .

"How abstractly furiating!" he howled, staring at the pond. He was so bothered and bewildered that his toes ventured too near to the edge and carried him screaming into the mud. "Aaaaggghhh!" he screamed, and beat at the sludge with his fists. "Look at me," he moaned. "Now I'll have to wash all my bodything! Get me out! Get me out!" And Anya dragged him out and got a beating for her pains. Oh yes, the Troll's fall cost the poor girl dear. That night, she could not sleep for the colors on her back from the Contradiction Stick. All night she sobbed from its blacks and blues. And while she wept the wicked Troll raged. He raged and raged until by morning he had devised a new task. An impossible task. Back he dragged her to where the pond had been, muttering darkly, yanking on the chain.

"Good," he said sourly. "Very good, very brilliant. You've dried the pond wetless. Oh yes, rather ingenious, don't know how." Anya said nothing, but held her breath in fear of what was to come. The Troll scowled at the mud. "Now," he said, baring his teeth, "you may build me a palatial. With numersome rooms and fully décored. All the bits, all the pieces, by nightfall. Or else." And off he scurried leaving Anya chained to the tree with a palace to build by nightfall. She could hear his snigger and cackle for a mile down the lane.

Hours later, she'd moved a single rock a few inches. The strain of it. The pain of it. But still she struggled, refusing to give up. Light was failing into the red and gray streaks of evening when the Lion appeared. He watched the poor girl lift and drop, lift and drop, lift and drop her pile of stones. "You're tired, my little," came his sonorous tones. "Why not rest a while?" Anya sighed. "Oh, Lion, I dare not, for my Lord the Troll will beat me until there is not a breath left in my body."

"Sh-h-h," murmured the Lion, his gentle mane shaking. "Sleep." And sleep she did, for his eyes lulled her, his presence soothed her, his voice rocked her gently into dreams.

She thought she was dreaming. The Troll had returned and was roaring at her. "How?" he was roaring. "How? How? How?" I must wake up, she thought. I must wake up. And she willed her eyes open to escape from the fearful rage. There he was, her Lord and Master, crouching over her, the bile spilling from him, his face a furious red, his teeth grinding. "How? How? How?" he was bellowing, shaking her until her head ached. Anya began to apologize, tried to explain that she'd fallen asleep, could not have managed his impossible task, when suddenly she saw it: a palace behind them, beautiful spires tearing the dark heavens, a perfect palace where before a pond had been. "How beautiful!" she cried. "How lovely!"

The Troll's nostrils twitched. "So," he began, the three thick fingers of each hand squeezing her arms, "it wasn't you who's done this?" Anya cowered. "No, sir." Triumph stretched the Troll's queer mouth into what passed for a smile. "Well, that's a contradiction," he smirked. "And when there is being a contradiction we should fetch our friend. Is that not the case?" Anya was wretched. "I don't know," she whispered. "Probably." The Troll skipped and lurched, all excited. "Very probably. Certain, in fact."

The Troll dragged Anya by the chain toward the palace. The huge walls, the stained glass, the soaring spires loomed above them. "This is more like it for an important Troll," he announced, and danced across the drawbridge. Inside they found delights of all descriptions. Walls hung with tapestries, chandeliers of crystal, goblets of gold, and rooms of many colors. In a Great Hall, a fire blazed, and the long table groaned with plate upon plate of a fabulous feast. The Troll's eyes rolled in his head, his lips drooled, his feet jigged. "Good! Yum! Mmmmm! Lovely!" he cackled, skipping around the food, dipping in, nibble-nibble, slurp-slurp. "And what about wine?" he asked, hitching Anya's chain to a ring in the wall and settling down to gorge himself. The glasses and jugs seemed empty. "I must have wine and sweet sherry," complained the Troll, happy to have something to be unhappy about. "Is there being a celery for wine?" His eyes darted about and came upon a cupboard. "Go and be seeing," he ordered his servant. "Try that door."

Anya went toward the door, but the chain pulled her up short a few feet from her destination. The Troll, a whole chicken bulging out his cheeks, the grease dribbling from the corners of his mouth, scurried over. "If you want something doing," he spluttered, bits of chicken trailing behind him, "be doing it yourself." He reached the door, opened it, and peered into the dark. "Let me fetch you a light," offered Anya, hurrying to the table where the candles flickered. The Troll puffed up with conceit. "A Troll can see perfectly clarified!" he told her, and walked into the shadows. Anya heard a terrible cry, which dropped away from her, echoing into the bowels of the palace, as the Troll fell and fell and landed with a dreadful thump.

Anya, horrified, ran to the door, but again the chain held her back. Straining at the chain, looking frantically about her, she saw the Lion appear from nowhere. "Oh, Lion, quick, quick!" she cried. "My Lord the Troll is in terrible trouble." The Lion pad-padded toward her. "I know," he said, and with a single flick of his paw shattered the chains that held her. Anya ran to the table, fetched a candle, and took it to the door. Holding the flame to the dark, she looked down and down. "Poor Troll," she whispered sadly. "No father nor mother and he was my other." The Lion's great head rubbed against her. "Not poor, my

little, but wicked and cruel. I made the palace. I also made the door."
And, saying this, he blew against the door, which vanished, the wall
closing up, leaving in its place a small portrait of the Troll.

And so Anya found herself mistress of the marvelous palace.
Upstairs dresses, downstairs food, servants everywhere. What a
transformation! One minute at the mercy of a wicked Troll, a Princess
the next. At the end of a long corridor, she found a room lined in
velvet, where beautiful gowns lay waiting for her. In the next chamber a hot bath drawn, rich with aromatic scents, and a sandalwood box
with pearls for her throat, diamonds for her ears, gold for her fingers.
Anya lay soaking away her past for hours and hours, and then dressed
herself, pinning up her hair. When, later, she walked back down the
corridor, passing a long gilt mirror, she blushed and curtsied, feeling
sure she had met a Princess, until she realized this beauty before her
was her own reflection. So she curtsied again, smiled, laughed,
danced. For the first time in her life, she felt wonderful.

And thus it was that a new life began for Anya. The days blessed
her, the nights caressed her, the weeks sailed peacefully into months,
and her beauty blossomed. And yet, beneath the silks and satins and
sun and servants, something ached, something yearned, something
pined in Anya's sweet heart. What Anya wanted was a Prince, or
someone very like a Prince, to share her blessed life with. And when
word spread of a lovely thing alone in a grand palace—well, they
flocked to her, the suitors, in droves: Prince La-Di-Dah of here, Prince
La-Di-Dah of there. But they were a little too much La, or a little too
much Di . . . or occasionally plain Dah! And a whole year went by
until the loneliness welled up in her and Anya began each morning
sighing at her window. She would have given everything—palace,
jewels, peace, everything—for the rush of blood, the pounding heart,
the song and the shudder that love brings.

Then, one day, as she listened to the larks, as she mooned upon the
terrace, she saw a tall youth bending to the roses, tending to the soil.
The sun touched his face and he whistled as he worked. All that

morning Anya watched him, and the next day, and the next, until she was ready before he came, heart pounding, the blood rushing to her cheeks. One morning, he looked up and smiled. Little fish swam up and down her back. And suddenly she wanted flowers in her room, flowers at her table, flowers for her hair, which he brought to her, smiling the while. And gradually the smiles turned to words, the words turned to whispers, and the whispers turned to kisses. She had fallen in love with the gardener. And why not? she told herself, full of song and shudder. She was a servant turned Princess. Why not a gardener turned Prince? Anya's heart did a little dance was all she knew. Each time she saw him, a little dance. And that was that. They talked and talked and talked. Marriage? Yes please. Children? Yes please. Happy ever after? Yes! "You are my True Bride," he told her, taking her in his arms. "Am I?" sighed Anya, kissing his cheek tenderly. "Then let no one else ever kiss your cheek." And her sweetheart touched the place where her lips had been and smiled. "Never," he vowed. "Never ever." For he loved her true and he loved her dear, and the future was surely roses and violets and daisies and definite.

Their wedding day beckoned. One morning, Anya's Beloved set off into the village. Appointments, he had, with the Tailor and the Barber and the Shoemaker. Spruced up, he would be, to marry his True Bride. She left him at the door, kissing his cheek, watching him go—his cheery wave, the sun following his steps—promising to count the minutes until he returned. And she did. She counted the minutes. She sat in her room, embroidering the silks and satins of her trousseau, and counted the minutes. Counted them into the hours when the lamps must be lit, counted them looking out from her balcony into the dark night, counted them straining to catch her Beloved returning, counted them in the creeping dawn as fear curdled her stomach, counted the minutes as they turned into days, as she sat at the table in her wedding dress, as the dust settled around her, as her heart broke, as the tears began to come. . . .

"I am his True Bride!" Anya cried to herself. "I am his True Bride!" But only the walls heard her, cold to her touch. She stopped counting the minutes, and once again the tear became her constant companion. And she never wound the clocks or sewed her trousseau or sang. Until, one day, she brushed the dust from her hair and summoned her resolve. She wrapped a cloak about her and stepped out into the world to find her sweetheart. She trudged to all points, through all weathers, but no luck, no sign, no clue. And so it was she found herself standing in the snow. And she knew she could go no farther.

"Anya? Anya?" She imagined in her sorrow she heard her name. And again, "Anya?" But looking about her, the snow swirling, she could see nothing, no one. And then, as if the snow itself were fashioning his shape, the Lion appeared, white in the white, his huge mane shaking, pad-padding toward her. Anya had no words, simply hugged and hugged him, the tears falling. He set her up on his back and leapt off, bounding through the snow, huge strides, impossible speeds, over cliff and cavern, crevasse and chasm, cave and canyon, helter-skelter to a strange land. A desert. And there, by a town, the Lion set her down. He must leave her, the Lion told her; she must finish the journey alone. Anya kissed his proud head and made ready to continue her search. Before he disappeared, the Lion dropped three

small walnuts onto the sand. "Take them," he said in his rich roar. "Take them. Inside there are gifts. Use them wisely." As Anya knelt to retrieve them, he disappeared, his body pouring into the sand. "Thank you, dearest Lion," whispered Anya to the sand. "I won't call for you again. And I will find my Beloved."

It was an hour later, as she approached a crossroads, that she saw people for the first time. Riders were approaching and Anya thought she would stop them to ask of her sweetheart, for why else had the Lion brought her to this strange place, unless to find him there? The riders neared, the sand billowing out under the hooves. The first horse cantered up to the crossroads, and Anya stepped out to greet the rider. Looking down at her, his face blank, his eyes clouded over, was her Beloved. . . .

"My Beloved!" cried Anya. "My darling!" The rider slowed his horse, tipped his hat, smiled politely, and rode on. "Wait!" she implored him. "Please wait!" But the horse continued without missing a stride. Before Anya could think what to do, the second rider was upon her. She turned. Her heart, in turmoil, missed one beat, then another. Her face went white. Her stomach churned. Fear seized her by the throat. For looking down at her from the saddle, with eyes rolling, was her Lord the Troll!

93

Anya fell backward, swooning, dumbfounded. She put up her hands, expecting any moment the thwish and thwack of the terrible stick to rain down on her. Nothing happened. She opened her eyes and saw the figure continuing on its way as if nothing had happened. Her eyes strained in the haze of the shimmering sand. And then she noticed a pigtail, a diamond earring, a hint of silk at the neck, and the truth hit her. It wasn't the Troll, it wasn't his ghost come to haunt her; it was his daughter the Trollop! Twice as ugly, twice as foul, and there she was, riding off with Anya's Beloved. He'd forgotten her! He didn't recognize her! She'd walked the wide world to find him and he'd forgotten her! Anya sank back to the ground and wanted the sand to swallow her as it had swallowed the Lion. She lay there, weeping, while the sun beat down on her. Then, slowly, slowly, her resolve strengthened. "I am the True Bride and he my Beloved!" she cried to the heavens. And without more ado she set off, determined.

On her way to the town, she met many folk, learned many things. One man told her that the Trollop, Queen of the sand, Mistress of the deserts, had traveled to the land of the Troll, her father. Another spoke how on the way she had met a handsome Prince and brought him back with her under the cast of a spell. Another told her they were betrothed. Each snippet tortured poor Anya, each clue tormented her. Her Beloved betrothed to another! Then, at the gates to the town, castle to the left, dungeons to the right, she met a woman.

"The Trollop's so greedy," whispered the woman, casting uneasy glances about her for fear of being heard. "Sees gold she wants it, silver she snatches it, diamonds, pearls, she'll give anything for jewels, covered she is in things precious, to hide what's underneath: a cruel heart, repugnant. She collects handsome men like ornaments. 'My Ornamen,' she calls them."

So instructed, Anya took a room for the night. A plan is what she needed, a plan to get back her man, and slowly, as she fell asleep, dizzy, spinning with the day's events, an idea came to her in a dream.

Next morning, she walked to the castle and stood under the Trollop's window. From her pocket, Anya took one of the Lion's gifts, cracking its shell against the wall. Sweet music—a lullaby harp—twinkled from it, and from one half of the walnut peeked a tiny piece of silk. Anya tugged on the silk, and inch by inch more material appeared, a continuous stream, unwinding and coiling on the ground around her. However she pulled, she could not reach the end of it, and after a while she was surrounded by the silk, swathed in its brilliant finery.

It wasn't long before the music threaded into the room where the Trollop sat. She scurried over to her terrace and looked down to see Anya with her fabulous treasure. "Hoy!" she called greedily. "That's being rather prettiness. I need it." Next minute, she was outside gathering up the silk, wrapping it around her shoulders, hugging it to her, wanting it.

Anya said nothing, but continued to draw the material from the walnut. "Is it being for peddle?" demanded the Trollop. "Is there a cost involved? I'm expecting it's a gift for your Queen, how kind and thank you." Anya smiled. "It's magic," she told the Trollop. "And therefore cannot be sold, only exchanged." And then she told her the bargain. She would give the Trollop the magic walnut in exchange for a night with the Prince. "With my new Ornaman?" exclaimed the Trollop, "Rageous!" Rageous or not, those were Anya's terms. The Trollop swooned in the silk. "Desperation," she mumbled, kissing the swathes of cloth. "I am delirious of it." And within a minute the bargain was struck. "How generous I'm being," she told Anya, snatching away the nut. "A night with my Ornaman. He's very sweetness, you know."

So it was that very evening the True Bride came to the castle to spend a night with her Beloved. "Alone," she told herself, heart racing. "Once alone, he'll know me." All atremble she entered his chamber, bathed in moonlight. Inside, asleep on his couch, was her darling. She rushed to him. At last! "My love!" she whispered gently, kneeling by him, "My love . . ." He did not stir. "Dearest," she sighed, taking his hand in hers. Nothing. The Prince slept and would not wake. "Please wake," she begged him. "It's me. Your True Bride." But no matter how she tried, no matter how she pleaded, his eyes stayed closed to her. No, the fact was he couldn't wake. A glass stood empty by his bed. In it, drunk nightly, was a sleeping herb, powerful, would last till morning. And when morning came, the bargain kept, Anya could do nothing but leave, her loved one none the wiser for her vain vigil. What could she do, our Anya, what could she do but try again?

Later the same day, the Trollop was sunning herself on the terrace, silk billowing, when she heard the sweet thread of Anya's music. In an instant, she was at the balcony squinting down to see Anya holding up one half of a walnut from which gold poured, impossibly, gold piece after gold piece, a small hill of gold already growing beneath her hand, and, accompanying the lullaby harp, she heard that marvelous tune which gold makes . . . chink, chink, chink, a fortune pouring onto the ground. The Trollop could not believe it. "Hoy!" she yelled. "I can't believe it!" And once again a night with the Beloved was swapped for Anya's magic. Quick, quick, the Trollop wanted the bargain struck, for there across the way, in the narrow slits that were the windows of the dungeons, gold was reflected in greedy eyes, gold blinked back from the jail's black holes.

But that night the same story. Anya hurried into her darling's chamber only for him to stay sleeping. "Darling," whispered his True Bride, over and over, and "Beloved." To no avail. Morning arrived and the Prince slept on, the cup of herbs beside him, two of Anya's gifts wasted. What could she do but try a final time?

As for the Prince himself, his days were vague, his nights dreamless. Stop him and ask him his thoughts, what would they be? "Oh," he'd murmur vaguely, or "Well . . ." The Trollop had rubbed away his past with her wicked spell. He hadn't heard his True Bride whispering the night through, weeping in the morning.

But the prisoners in the dungeon had listened, their eyes blinking in the black, their ears sharp. Yes, they'd heard the clink of gold, but also the True Bride's lament. So the next day when the Prince was walking the ramparts, they called out to him. "How can you sleep at night," they cried, "with the beauty weeping at your side?" The Prince looked out at the sheer granite walls of the dungeons, the narrow slits crowded with faces. " 'Beloved,' she calls you," they told him. "And says she is your True Bride." The Prince scratched his head, his past denied him, his memory a cloud. "When do you hear these things?" he asked them. "All night. All night," they chorused. "Oh," murmured the Prince. "Well . . ." And he walked on, bewildered.

But even as he walked, the Queen of all the sand, Mistress of all the deserts, was hovering on her terrace, ears twitching in readiness, eyes swiveling. Yes! There it was, the harp's sweet lullaby. And another sound . . . like a chandelier shivering in the wind. She rushed down the stairs, not bothering to look over the balcony, hurtled down, silk cascading, gold chinking, charged to the spot under her window where Anya stood with the third gift, a rain of diamonds and rubies, sapphires and emeralds pouring to the ground in a torrent. The Trollop was close to fainting with greed. "Oh! oh! oh!" she sighed, her little legs buckling beneath her, the jewels glittering in her gaze. "So meeable, so agreeable! I need them!" Her tiny anxious eyes darted about her. From the narrow slits of the dungeons she saw the jewels reflected. "Quick! Quick!" she urged Anya. "Gather up all my little babies. Eyes being everywhere . . . hurry!"

So the bargain was struck for the third time. Something for nothing, smirked the Trollop to herself, hanging diamonds from her ears, pinning them to her silks. And that night Anya arrived for her vigil, the final gift gone, her Beloved sleeping deeply. "Will you never wake?" she lamented, despairing at the sleeping Prince. She took his hand and wept as the precious minutes ticked away, her tears marking the seconds. "Don't cry." Anya dropped his hand in shock. Her darling had waked! "Don't cry," he murmured again, forcing himself from sleep. "Dearest," wept Anya. "My dearest." But the Prince did not recognize her. "Oh," he murmured vaguely. "Well . . ." Anya leaned over to kiss his cheek but he shrank away. "Not there," he said, unease clouding his eyes. "I promised, you see, not there."

"Me!" Anya told him. "Me! You promised me!" And with that she kissed him and the Trollop's spell over him fell away, and his head cleared, such a tender kiss, such love, such sweetness of cheek. "My True Bride," he whispered. "My True Bride!"

At that very same moment in the vaults of the castle, where the Trollop sat counting the piles of gold, a strange thing happened. Very odd. The silks, an armada of them draping the Trollop, faded and shriveled, dropping from her in tatters. The jewels, pinned everywhere, disintegrated into sand, sand pouring from her ears, her neck, her wrists, her fingers. And the coins, barrels of gold, crumbled to dust before her. "Aarrggh!" howled the Trollop. "No! My goldies! My silknesses! My die-dies! Come back!" And she began to jump and skip and hop and stumble and buckle and foam and bellow like a bull. In she burst to the Beloved's chamber, her rage booming down the corridor. But too late—the couple had fled.

Oh yes, too late! They've gone, they're away, the lovers, running, running, running home together. The Trollop, apoplectic with anger, sent dogs, men, cannon, sent her whole army in their wake. "After them! Get them back! Whiz! Haste! Hurtle!" And the Trollop herself pursued them, hissing, spitting poison, cursing, cantering across the desert. Charged by bile, fueled by thunder, she closed on the fleeing couple, until she must surely catch them. Anya and her Beloved heard her galloping legs approaching, the baying of dogs, the gnashing of teeth nearer and nearer. "Gggrrrrrr!" roared the Trollop, planning their punishment, ripping them limb from limb in her mind. She was on them, her hot breath on their backs, shrieking in triumph when, suddenly, rising from the sand itself, the great white Lion appeared, growling, forcing her to a halt. On his back the couple clambered, and off he sped while the hapless Trollop was forced to watch, hopeless. Yes, off he sped, bounding through the sand, bounding through the snow, impossible speeds, over cliff and cavern, crevasse and chasm, cave and canyon, helter-skelter to the palace. Home!

"Thank you, Lion!" they cried, hugging him, locking the doors, catching their breath, thrilled, delighted, their adventure over. And they lit a fire and exchanged their stories, how the one was enchanted, the other despairing. And in between, hugs; and all the time, kisses; while the Lion tossed back his proud mane and padded away, leaving the lovers, but not before a final task, unseen. The lovers, for their part, barely noticed he had gone, they were so full of their past, their present, and their future. They were home, they were safe, they were sound, the care falling away from them. So it was that they quite forgot about the Trollop, who had not forgotten them. Even as they blew out their candles and prepared to sleep, she was well past cliff, well past cavern, long past the crevasse, and hurdling the chasm . . .

and getting nearer. By the time the True Bride and her Beloved were deep in dream, she had arrived, stealthy as a bat, at the doors to the palace, determined to exact a dreadful vengeance.

She scurried inside, sniffing them out, her nostrils twitching and heaving. There! her nose told her. There! behind the door. And, inching toward it, sure enough, she heard their voices, heard their laughter, her evil smile spreading over the bulging teeth, her hands moist with excitement. With a roar and a leap she charged at the door, leaping in . . . and fell.

And no sooner had she landed with a terrible thud than the hole closed up and the door disappeared. Upstairs the lovers slept on peacefully. And from that day lived peacefully. Babies came to bless them and the sun forever shone, and on their wall they hung a painting of the Lion, whom they both called the Thought Lion. And they explained to their children he could come alive in an instant if he wanted to, or if they needed him. But the children found it hard to believe.

Fearnot

SNAKES for some, spiders for others. Or the dark: black cold pitch, full of secrets. Or being high up: dizzy, eyes screwed shut against the drop. There are those for whom it is small rooms, no windows, the walls squeezing out the air. For some it is vast open spaces, endless horizons, the heart thumping to find home. The list goes on and on. All of us are frightened of something. Bats, bulls, beards, blood, buttons, slugs, cobwebs, crabs, caterpillars, cellars, fire, water, lightning, thunder—any of these can start the cold prickly sweat, the heart stop, the shiver, and the shudder. And the only remedy for a bad case of the shudders is to tell yourself the story of the boy who set forth to learn what fear was.

Now he was a rare boy. The second son of the second cousin of my second wife's second niece, who'd died and left her husband—a Tailor—with two sons, the one good, the other good for nothing. And this latter boy was called Fearnot, and he played the fiddle and folk found him a fine fool of a fellow.

Picture him: a shock of red hair, a fixed grin, a light heart, and cheeks spattered with freckles. He had no trade and no wish for one. Nothing suited him better than to sit with his fiddle and scrape out tunes, idling away the afternoons with a song and a smile. Best of all, he liked to find a spot underneath the window of his sweetheart—a Merchant's daughter, a beauty, a darling—and serenade her, coaxing a shy wave from her slender hand, a lovely laugh from her cupid lips. Oh yes, this was best fun, until the father appeared, all flush-cheeked and furious, flinging down flowerpots at the fiddling Fearnot. "Be off!" he'd say. "Good-for-nothing!" And he'd be right on that count, for if Fearnot wasn't valued for his forever smile or his dancing fiddle, why then he was indeed of little worth to the wide world.

One day, soaked through from a rainy spell of sweet reels under his sweetheart's window, a smile as long as tomorrow, Fearnot skipped home to find his father and his brother hard at work, their fingers flying through the stitches. The Tailor looked up, all thumb and thimble, his face dark with rage.

"What time do you call this?" he demanded, scowling at his son. Fearnot was confused. "I don't know, Father," he replied, smiling. "What time do you call it?" His father sighed a sigh, his eyes rolling heavenward. "God give me patience!" he exclaimed, then thought better of his temper. "Have you got the buttons?" Buttons? Fearnot didn't know what his father was talking about. "The buttons I sent you out for this morning!" exploded the Tailor. Fearnot beamed in recollection. "Do you know, Dad," he said genially, "I complete forgot them buttons. I stood and played under my sweetheart's window. She's a lovely."

Exasperation forced his father's eyebrows up to his scalp. He turned to his other son and ordered him out to get the buttons. But the elder son, as normal as Fearnot was odd, was frightened of the journey. The walk home would take him through the forest after dark, and he was fearful of the shadows. There were trolls there, and dragons. At the mention of the word "dragon," Fearnot piped up. "Let me go," he said. "I don't mind shadows and I never saw a dragon." The Tailor nodded wearily, one son fearful, the other frightful. Fearnot grinned and gamboled for the door. "What are you going for?" tested his father. Fearnot couldn't quite remember. "Don't tell me," he said, scratching his head. "To see dragons—?" Father's face went crimson.

Fearnot tried again. "No. Uh, ogres — ?" Father erupted, his voice volcanic. "BUTTONS!" he bawled. "BUTTONS!"

Fearnot's smile stretched until it seemed it might meet at the back of his head. "Buttons," he repeated, setting off into the night, saying the word over and over in case he forgot again.

"Buttons," memorized Fearnot as he skipped his way through the village and threaded his way through the forest, eyes skinned for a troll or dragon or curiosity, but he saw none, made his way to the town, remembered the buttons, and set off on the journey home, a thousand of them jingling in a big leather purse. As he passed the square, he beamed his twice-round-the-head smile at a gaggle of youths who loafed and lingered on the lookout for mischief. A mischief of youths, you might say. They stared their violent stare, laconic eyes following Fearnot as he headed for the forest. One greasy head bent to the next and muttered. The next head guffawed and bent to the third, passing on the jape. Then all three smirked and slipped from their posts and into the woods.

The evening was growing dark. Moans, howls and hoots, and the sudden creak of branches lent a sinister music to Fearnot's journey. None of this affected him in the slightest. Quite the reverse. He had his fingers crossed for a surprise. He kept to the shadows, hoping to stumble on a snoozing nasty of one sort or another. That would be a good story for his brother! But he was out of luck, it seemed, as he neared the edge of the forest. Then, suddenly, a huge shape reared in front of him.

"GGGGGRRRR!" it roared, looming monstrously above him. "Hello!" cried Fearnot, excited. "What are you? A troll?" The monster bellowed back, swaying ominously. "I am a Wurdle!" it bellowed. "Only twice as bad." "Never mind," Fearnot sympathized. The Wurdle lurched forward. "I want your bag of buttons," it demanded in a new voice. Fearnot apologized and explained they were for his dad. The Wurdle growled. "Give them to me or I'll reduce you!"

Fearnot asked the monster to explain. "I'll mutton you!" it threatened in yet another voice. "I'll give you a right flummox!" Fearnot was not familiar with any of these terms, but decided they didn't sound very nice. "That doesn't sound very nice," he said. "Give me the buttons!" the monster stormed, all voices sounding in a terrible chorus. Fearnot frowned and swung the bag of buttons. "Very well," he said, and dealt the Wurdle a resounding blow across the chops, sending it flying. As the monster fell, it seemed to come apart, like a troupe of collapsing acrobats, and before Fearnot could say "Fol-de-rol," the mischief of youths from the square had run off bruised and battered into the woods, butt of their own jape.

Fearnot hardly noticed the revelation. He was too busy trying to rescue a button or two from the scattered bag. After an hour he had eleven.

Back went our boy to his dad's house, full of tales of a Wurdle, only twice as bad, and sorry about the buttons, and did you know a Wurdle has three voices, quite remarkable, eh? And his dad, reduced, muttoned, flummoxed by this Wurdle of his own flesh, could stomach it no longer and set his son outside, handed him fifty shillings in a purse, and told him to go off, for pity's sake, and learn something! Fearnot considered this strange mission and nodded. He'd always wanted to learn how to shudder, he told his father. The knack of it had eluded him. Yes, he declared, he would set forth to learn what fear was. Did Dad think that was a good idea? Anything, cried the Tailor, his eyes rolling to the heavens. Anything. Fearnot grinned happily. Then that's what I'll do, he announced, and straight off he went without bag or bun or a second thought. Father stood and watched him, shaking his head as his son waltzed off, for he was a rare boy and no mistake. Off he went, rolling into the world with nothing to guide him but a bag of shillings, a fiddle, and a fool's errand. Many of us have done the same.

And so the boy set forth to learn what fear was, and he looked for it in many a dark place, under many an upturned stone; oh yes, he

walked and walked until at length he came—as at length you must—
to a crossroads. And there he met a man. Not an ordinary man, mark
you, but a ragtag-and-bobtail of a fellow—a Tinker, to be sure, with
a leprechaun's face and an undertaker's coat and a belt rattling with the
oddest objects, pots, pans, potions, relics, and tools of the most
mysterious trades. Seeing Fearnot approaching, this Mr. Jingle Jangle beamed a Celtic beam, dusted down his breeches causing an
explosion of dust, and sneezed and achooed! his way toward him.

"Good day, young man!" he announced with a toothless flourish.
"Now here's a lucky meeting." Fearnot agreed and said so. One
eyebrow on the Tinker's face arched knowingly. "Ah, I can see by the
gleam in your eye you have a sweetheart," he observed with a cackle.
"I do, sir," acknowledged our boy, intrigued. "What's her name?"
asked the Tinker. Fearnot didn't know, he was sorry. The Tinker
shrugged. "Ach, what's a name, I always say. Mine's McKay and I
don't mind it." "Mine is Fearnot," said Fearnot. Mr. McKay nodded a
sage nod. "And there you are, as my poor mother would say. Do you
have a mother?" Fearnot shook his head. "I'm afraid I don't."

"Still, we all had one once and that's the main thing," the Tinker
told Fearnot, and patted him on the back in consolation. Then he
began to produce all manner of trinkets from his carpet bag. "Tell
me," he urged his young friend, "is your sweetheart dark or fair?"
"Dark," Fearnot told him. "Like Arabia." Mr. McKay seemed delighted. "Like Arabia!" he exclaimed, hopping from one foot to the
other. "Happy day! A happy day for you, young fellow-me-lad. For I
have in my bag a scarf of silk direct from the shores of Arabi." And
with this he produced a scarf and dangled it in front of our boy.
"Here," he said, waving the scarf under Fearnot's nose. "Take it, and
may you learn a name with it." Fearnot felt its silk softness. "Thank
you," he said, over and over. "Thank you!" The Tinker adopted the
tone of a generous soul. "Because I can see you're a good fellow," he
began, "I'm only going to ask from you what I paid myself. A double
Persian."

Fearnot had no idea how much even a single Persian might amount to. "How much is that?" he inquired. "How much do you have?" came the instant reply. "Fifty shillings," Fearnot told him, for that was how much he had. Mr. McKay had an attack of the coughing. When he recovered, he seemed quite unimpressed by the figure. "Nothing like that much," he said, waving away with his hand. "Oh no, barely half," he muttered. "Less than two-thirds." His eyebrow seemed to twist into a private question mark. Fearnot, for his part, was thinking past this transaction. "I'd like the scarf," he told his new friend, "because I have set forth to learn things, and to learn a name is, I suppose, something. But I'll give you all I have if you could but teach me what fear is."

Now both of the Tinker's eyebrows quizzed and quivered. One curled into the figure 5, the other to an O. He asked Fearnot if it were really true, he would give fifty shillings for the favor of frightening him? Fearnot nodded earnestly. Mr. McKay seemed deep in thought, chin tucked into his chest. Fearnot waited. Suddenly the Tinker launched at him, roaring. "Is something the matter?" asked Fearnot in a concerned voice. Mr. McKay shook his head and thought of another tack.

"Close your eyes," he said, at last. Fearnot obliged, shutting them tight. At this, the Tinker pulled a knife from his bag and set its cold blade against the boy's young throat. "What do you think I have at your throat?" he asked in a menacing voice. Fearnot shrugged. "A knife?" "That's right," hissed the Tinker. "A sharp knife. It will split a hair clean in two." Fearnot, eyes closed, seemed impressed. "It can slice a throat without touching the sides," continued the Tinker. "That's a good knife, then," declared Fearnot, patiently waiting for something to happen. "It certainly is," agreed Mr. McKay. "And will slice yours, young man, unless you give me your bag of shillings," and with this he let the knife press into Fearnot's proffered flesh. "I can't do that!" laughed Fearnot, thumping Mr. McKay heartily and sending him flying to the ground, pots and pans and bits and bones

106

scattering. "For I must learn what fear is and I'm not frightened of you, Mr. McKay, you're a friend!"

The Tinker scrabbled to his feet, gathering up his possessions. "No, that's right," he said ruefully. "We're friends. I'm sure we are." He rubbed his rump with a grimace. "No," he sighed, "let me take you down the lane and then I think I can arrange a small case of the shudders for you." And, hobbling and clanking, he hurried off, head buzzing, Fearnot following. "Where are we going?" inquired the young man. The Tinker pointed to the horizon. "To a pond by a hedge by a field by a mill by a town. And in that pond is a fearful sight. So fearful," he said gravely, "think what fearful is, and add ten." Fearnot was delighted. "And shall I shudder?" he wanted to know, his voice brimming with excitement. "No question," replied the Tinker and hurried on, adding under his breath, "If you survive . . ."

So off they set, a most fanciful perigrination, until they came at last to a pond by a hedge by a field by a mill by a town. And as they arrived with day ending, they saw folk rushing from the mill, still dusted with flour, and these souls would not stop to swap words, shouting instead as they hurried off, "Be clear before dark falls!" "Beware the pond!" And other such unwelcomes. Fearnot was somewhat bewildered by these exhortations until Mr. McKay pointed out that they were encouraging signs of the shuddering to come. It was the pond, he explained, with its terrible secret that would do the trick for Fearnot, and that was why the squeamish had fled. Mr. McKay himself seemed anxious not to loiter, looking fretful at the sky as the sun dropped, bringing with it the pink and gray cloths of evening. "Plunge into the pond," he told the boy in a curiously contradictory gait, one foot moving toward the bank, the other restless to depart. "Fear will swim up to greet you." "Splendid," declared his charge, busy removing his boots.

By now, Mr. McKay was extremely nervous. "Good, good," he muttered uncomfortably. "I'll retire and find us beds for the night. You must sleep after a good fright." With that, he slipped the purse of shillings from Fearnot's possession, then hurried off, sending puffs of encouragement over his shoulder as he scampered away. All alone, Fearnot paddled, his feet stirring the green waters, waiting for something frightful to happen. . . .

Now this pretty pond was not all welcome-cool and water lilies. Deep in its green deep was a monster, a Terrible Thing, and the Terrible Thing was disturbed by splashes. It peered up through the green and saw a pair of feet. And had Fearnot been down in the depths, he would have heard the sound of stirrings and an indignant rumbling. But he wasn't, so he didn't. Instead, he sat dangling his feet in the pond, waiting to shudder, wondering how, when all of a sudden and who would believe it, the water began to gather and froth and swirl—as if lifting up a lacy petticoat—and blow me if a ring of sad beauties didn't appear, set a-dancing, eyes closed and melancholy.

These were the Sisters of the Deep, lost daughters in the service of the monster, water in their eyes, water in their veins, their dance a welcome to drowning. Come in, come in, they seemed to say . . . come in and sip our bitter beer. And Fearnot looked on, enchanted by their loveliness as they swam in intricate patterns an inch below the surface, beguiling, entrancing, all grace and invitation. But instead of joining them, he did what he always did when the mood took him. He pulled out his fiddle and began to play. A sweet old reel. A ragadoon. And, hearing his music, the beauties opened their liquid eyes and moved to its coaxing lilt. So it went on, Fearnot fiddling, dancers dancing, until suddenly the pool churned and agitated and from the gushing green the monster emerged, a thing of slime and seaweed, half-man, half-lobster, all tendrils and tentacles, eyes rolling on waving stalks.

Now why did the village folk avoid this pretty scene? Why did men tremble at nightfall as the moon gleamed its silver on the pool? Because this green creature in its coat of slime puncturing the surface, this Terrible Thing swimming toward Fearnot and his music, had but

two sports: to drown men and to drown women. He reared up at
Fearnot, dripping and dreadful. "Do you know who I am?" he
demanded in a voice choked with tiny fish. Fearnot shrugged. "I don't
think so," he said politely. "You're not a Wurdle." He thought a bit.
"Some sort of Terrible Thing?" The monster's eyes rotated on their
stalks. "Exactly," he spluttered. "These are my pretties. They tempt
young men like you and I drown them." Before Fearnot could

ask why, the monster continued, hypnotized by the fiddle and its sweet song.

"Sell me your bird," he said dreamily. Fearnot tried to explain that it wasn't a bird, that it was a box with strings, that he made the song with his bow, but the monster would not believe him. He splashed out of the water, a thing of stem and stalk, huge and ugly. Others would have fled for their lives; Fearnot merely looked, eyes wide with curiosity, enjoying this adventure. The Terrible Thing approached him, flailing, but it was not the boy he wanted but the magic bird. His webbed hand scraped the fiddle, and the strings screeched and jangled. "Horrible!" mourned the monster, disappointed. "You must learn to play it," said Fearnot sympathetically, and demonstrated the fiddle's true voice.

Tears leaked from the monster's eyes. "Your bird!" he cried. "Where does its song come from?" "Faraway," Fearnot told him. "Ireland." The monster's eyes swiveled the possible directions. "Which way is Ireland?" he asked. Fearnot looked to the west, to where the hills stretched out in a long procession. "Over there," he said, pointing to the hills. "Many lefts. Many rights." The monster looked to the west with a look of yearning. "Then I'll go there," he spluttered. "Ireland." And off he dripped, the green tears raining from him, leaving his daughters and his pool and his endless drowning, slithering away in search of Ireland and the bird that sings. For all I know, he lives there now.

Next morning, the mischievous McKay had a rude shock. There he was, fifty golden shillings in his pocket and doing a fine trade in relics and rosaries—for this was a village of many funerals—when along came Fearnot in a fine rage, indignant at the theft of his shillings and if not disgruntled, certainly not gruntled. Oh no, not gruntled in any way at all. He stormed through the eager crowd of customers, and set about the miserable Tinker, berating and bewailing him, and would have made tomato of his nose and cauliflower of his ear had he not revealed the sum of his exploits and the fate of the Terrible Thing.

Through his rant and rail, the crowd caught on, and next minute hoisted our boy up and carried him aloft through the streets, circled ten times around the pond, then back for a carnival that did not stop for a week.

Later, after not one feast but twenty, seventy-eight gifts, four offers of marriage, and much playing of the fiddle, the whole village collapsed into bed and slept soundly, freed from the terror of the Terrible Thing. By then, Mr. McKay, self-appointed manager of heroes, and historian of Fearnot's exploits, had noted details of trolls and terrors and dragons and demons and untold unsolved mysteries. Thus commissioned, the two companions set off, cheers still ringing in their ears, and it wasn't until late the following day, heads still muddled with cider, that Fearnot remembered to clap the Tinker's ears, retrieve his fifty shillings, and ask him where they were heading next.

Mr. McKay, possessed of a map of many colors, turned it round and round in study. His lip, pendulous at the best of times, positively drooped after Fearnot's thrashing. "Well," he said sulkily, "I have here the route to a fine terror, but I must have reward." Fearnot reminded him of the promise of the shillings once he was properly frightened. Mr. McKay looked peevish. "You promise me much, but give me only your fist, which I like not!" On he went, muttering and mumbling, bemoaning his lot. "I try, I try," he muttered, "then one little misunderstanding and I am thrashed for my pains." And so they proceeded, Fearnot pulling their donkey loaded up with the seventy-eight gifts, Mr. McKay ahead, nose in the map, cussing and cursing, his belt of pots, pans, and paraphernalia jingling and jangling with each step he took. "Compare us," he continued. "You are blessed with a great courage. I am cursed with a little cunning. I cheat for trifles, you can move mountains! Is that fair, I ask you?"

Now Fearnot felt pity for the Tinker and held out the bag of shillings. But the Tinker would not take it. "No, no," he insisted moodily. "I'll struggle on for nothing. I'll guide you," and, pointing

to the horizon, he picked out a spiky silhouette perched on a peak. "We go to a castle where none can survive a night. That sounds an impossible task and will therefore suit you." Fearnot put a hand to his brow and squinted at the castle. "So I will learn to shudder at last?" he asked hopefully. The Tinker shrugged. "We can but hope," he said.

Now the castle they approached was a graveyard of hopes. There it stood on the horizon, a place brooding. Enchanted, the King driven out, the rooms abandoned, only fools sought shelter there. For they had reached a troubled land where bad held sway. But fools there were, as always, tempted by the fabled store of fabulous treasure.

Suddenly the ground crunched underfoot and, looking down, Mr. McKay let cry a fearful shriek, for at his boot was a skull, and next to it another, and next to that another, and so on, stretching out before them, a path of grim bones, all that was left of their predecessors. Mr. McKay was terrified. "Bones," he whispered. Fearnot pressed on and looked down into the wide mouth of the moat. Dark liquid filled it. Fearnot investigated. "Blood," he announced. Before the Tinker had time to suggest they might try a smaller shudder but a few miles distant, an ungodly moan issued from the castle, and the drawbridge swung open with a mighty crash. Fearnot was delighted. "Wait here," he told his partner, and rummaged through the gifts. "I should take something with me." Mr. McKay was paralyzed with fear. "Take a sword," he suggested. "Take two." But Fearnot ignored his advice, and decided, instead, on a small grinding wheel. "This will be enough," he declared. "Or not, as the case may be. And it leaves you seventy-seven of my gifts, should I never return."

The Tinker was down in the mouth. "Do not leave them here," he pleaded. "You know how it is with me. I will be forced to steal them and desert you." Fearnot smiled a nice smile, and took his friend's arm. "Have a little courage, Mr. McKay," he said, and with that he turned and hurried into the dark bowels of the castle. A second hideous cry greeted his entrance. Mr. McKay was beside himself with dread. "A little courage, Mr. McKay," he reminded himself, and stood shivering by the drawbridge.

The hall of the castle was vast and dark. Fearnot found gnarled candles whose wax had long since wept onto the floor, chairs lonely with dust, a long table heavy with secrets, and everywhere a silence with eyes that watched his every move, with ears that heard his every step. The only sounds were tiny creaks, furtive scurries, and the wind keening through the shattered windows. Oh yes, in the cold hearth of the fireplace, fear sat, invisible, and waited. . . . Even brave men could not stay in this place, but Fearnot wandered about with a hop and a skip, dipping into dust, eager-beaver for some action. And it came. For suddenly, without warning, a gust billowed from the chimney and after it, with a bellow, appeared a man—or, more precisely, half a man, for there was nothing at all below his waist.

No one seemed more surprised at this than the man himself. "Hello," he said, astonished. "There's only half of me here." And, ignoring Fearnot, he levered himself on his hands to peer anxiously up from whence he had come. "Where's the rest of me?" he demanded in a voice booming with anger. Fearnot had never seen a more ugly sight than this Half-Man with his severed legs. His head seemed to have nothing to do with his neck, his arms less to do with his body. For all the world, he looked as if he had been hastily thrown together from bits of other people. And indeed he had.

While Fearnot looked on, astonished, the Half-Man dragged his miserable trunk around the floor, roaring with rage, until once more the chimney belched and this time issued forth a pair of legs, jerking and twitching. The Half-Man let out a satisfied growl, scraped his way back to the hearth, and in a second had hauled himself up onto these limbs. Thus attached and apparently satisfied, he took a few cautious steps, legs leading, body catching up in a quadrille of discord. The Half-Man shook his head and muttered, thumping at his new legs in disgust. "These aren't my legs!" he announced accusingly to the bewildered Fearnot. "These are definitely not my legs!"

Fearnot shrugged, feeling unable to comment on what belonged to this man and what didn't. Instead, he offered his best smile and introduced himself. The Half-Man eyed him curiously. "How about a game?" he asked, licking his lips at the prospect. "Why not?" replied Fearnot. "I have all night." This response brought such a guffaw from the man it threatened to detach his heaving belly from his bottom half. "He has all night!" he roared, most amused. Then he stomped over to a chest and yanked it open to reveal a collection of bones.

"Skittles!" he explained gleefully, and set about arranging them in

a clump at one end of the hall, thrusting the great table aside with a single flick of his wrist. "Good!" he declared, eyes gleaming. "Now what size legs are those?" he demanded, pointing a ferocious finger at Fearnot's lower half. Fearnot didn't know, and said so. Half-Man frowned and stumped closer for a thorough investigation. "No gout?" he queried. Fearnot shook his head. "Corns? Blisters? Foot rot?" continued his interrogator. "No," said Fearnot, wondering where this line of questioning might lead. "Good, good," mumbled the Half-Man. "I could do with those legs, these are too short by half."

And with that he dipped back into the chest and produced a skull, then staggered to the opposite end of the hall where he took aim at the skittles. "You'd better win, precious!" he cried, announcing the stakes. "Else you'll find yourself half the man you were!" At this, he hurled the skull at the bones, sending eight of them flying into the air. "Eight!" he cried, triumphantly punching the air. "Eight! Not bad on borrowed legs." Folding at the waist, he reset the skittles, delivering the skull with such force to Fearnot that he was knocked sideways, collapsing into a heap. "Careful," warned the Half-Man. "Don't want them pegs damaged!"

Fearnot picked himself up and carried the skull over to the grinding wheel. "You won't mind, sir," he said, "but your ball is not round enough for me," and so saying he brought bone to blade in an excruciating grind. In a few seconds the skull was perfectly round, and Fearnot, full of intent, aimed at the skittles. His throw was powerful and true, the ball hurtling toward the bones with a smooth and deadly flourish. Up jumped the bones, every one of them, dancing in the air before scattering across the hall. "Aaargh!" howled the Half-Man. "You cheated!" "No, sir," replied Fearnot. "I swapped a little courage for a little cunning!" But the Half-Man was inconsolable, for even as Fearnot spoke, the legs pulled away from the body and lurched off toward the fireplace. The Half-Man himself, legs abandoning him, crashed to the floor and disappeared before Fearnot's eyes.

Outside, Mr. McKay, temptation nibbling at his resolve, picked through the lucky dip of presents. He found a beautiful goblet studded with jewels and held it up for the moon's approval. Then a silver plate and a diamond ring. "Lovely," he murmured, greed goading. "All lovely." The wind howled around him, blood gushed into the moat, screams curled from the castle. He shivered. Run, said the little demons in his head, run, run, run.

Inside, Fearnot—for want of a fright—settled down for the night. He found a bed piled thick with velvet eiderdowns, and slipped underneath them. His legs nudged something cold. Pulling back the plump covers, he met with a dreadful sight. Lying there, eyes closed, no pulse, no breath, was his friend and companion, Mr. McKay. "Oh, mister," cried Fearnot, sad in his heart, "is it all up with you?" The Tinker did not move. Tenderly, Fearnot touched his forehead. "So cold," he sorrowed. "You were my first and only friend." Grief and dismay welled up in Fearnot as he carried the Tinker into the dark hall and built up a fire in the grate. As the meager flames dipped and danced, he held the limp body over them, wrapped in the velvet cover, and tried to warm him back to life.

Just as sorrow was teasing a tear from the corners of his eyes, Fearnot felt the slightest tremble from deep inside the velvet. He unwrapped the covers, excitement mounting, and pulled back the cloth. Staring at him with an evil leer was the face of the Half-Man! With a mighty roar the creature was upon him, thick fingers squeezing at his throat, a foul breath choking him. They fought, rolling over and over on the damp stone of the hall, growl and grimace, might and marrow. Now it was Fearnot forcing back his opponent, now it was the Half-Man cruel and crushing, threatening to tear the boy limb from limb. So it went on for an hour, this fearful wrestle, until at last, exhausted, with a final fling, Fearnot got the better of his adversary and dashed his head on the stone. There was a terrible crack as the Half-Man fell back and broke into a thousand pieces, dust and fragments flying into the air. One moment he was there, huge and murderous, the next he had disappeared in a swirl of sulphurous gas, back to the depths from which he had come. Fearnot lay on the flagstones, heart pounding, strength spent. The fire had long died and the hall was pitched into blackness.

"Fearnot?" came a small voice from the dark, and again, "Fearnot?" The giddy, swaying light of a torch flickered into the hall, casting a long shadow over Fearnot. Standing before him, trembling, was Mr. McKay, his tiny, anxious voice echoing against the stone. "Fearnot!" it pleaded, desperate.

Fearnot sprang up, no longer deceived by this hall of horror and its mischief. "Come nearer, demon," he cried, "and I will cut off your head, and then there will be three parts to marry!" "What?" came the timid reply. Fearnot was not fooled. "I know it is not you," he said, ready for the fray. "It *is* me!" insisted the man before him, blue eyes blinking. "Dead again, are you?" said Fearnot, tensing. Mr. McKay looked very offended. "No!" he said, and took a step toward our boy. Fearnot pulled out his knife, gleaming in the torch's flare, and swung it threateningly across the Tinker's path. The little man leapt back aghast. "Please!" he cried. "I'm terrified! I came with my little courage and it's quite used up."

Fearnot faltered. "How many gifts did I leave with you?" he quizzed. The Tinker frowned guiltily. "Well, I could only count seventy-seven to begin with and I ate two . . . well, two and half . . . but there's still plenty." But Fearnot was not convinced. "What's the name of my true love?" he asked, ready to lunge. Now the man looked very vexed. "How can I know if you don't?" he complained. And Fearnot knew it really was the Tinker and was overjoyed. "Then it *is* you!" "Of course it's me!" said Mr. McKay, most aggrieved. Delight danced on Fearnot's face. "And you came in to find me?" "And small thanks I get," the Tinker moaned. "It's my lot. I try to break the mold and be decent and I get a knife thrust at me." His friend was undeterred. "Come here," said Fearnot, "and hug me." "No," sulked the Tinker, then hugged him just the same.

Oh yes, hug him he did, and there the two friends stayed until morning while Fearnot told his tale and the Tinker told his, and pleased as punch they both were with themselves. Then they searched the castle from top to toe, and behind the farthest door of the highest floor they found a room, and in that room was gold, such goldness they might have thrown it out the window for a week and still be swamped. And they shared it half and half and a bit for luck, and never have two men danced more nor merrier. And from a distance you would have seen the castle shake off its gray drab and sunbathe.

Next day, the boon companions, weighed down with treasure, set off on their way and found themselves not far from Fearnot's village. A thousand thoughts haunted our hero as he walked. Why hadn't he learned to shudder? What could he tell his father? Where else could he look? Such conundrums consumed him as they rounded the ridge that led down to his long-left home, and how could it not be so, for is it not the point of adventures that you learn much but not the things you thought of?

At last they reached the gate, footsore and found. Fearnot pulled back the latch and beckoned his friend, but Mr. McKay shook his head. "We say goodbye, then," he said sadly. "But you must meet my family," protested Fearnot. "No, no," the Tinker told him. "Families never like me," and with that he reached inside his raggedy tunic and pulled out the leather purse of shillings. "What's this for?" asked Fearnot. "You must return it to your dad," explained Mr. McKay, "for you have not learned what fear is." And Fearnot took the purse and smiled and then pulled the little man to him and gave him a huge hug, and from one side you might have seen a tear in his eye, and from the other a tear in the Tinker's. Then he was off, Mr. McKay, his donkey loaded with half the bounty of their exploits. Fearnot watched him go, a jingle and a jangle, a jumble of mischief and twinkle, watched him struggle up the path and then turn on the horizon and wave, a wave that ran all the way back down the path to touch Fearnot's heart. "Goodbye, my friend," he whispered, and walked inside.

There he found things much as before, father and brother busy at the needle, thread flying back and forth. And you can imagine the look he got, for when last seen what an empty head he'd been, the boy who could not remember buttons. But how the sour turned sweet when he showed them both the gold, how the weary turned to wonder. And while son scooped sovereign after sovereign from the bulging sack, while dad dug into the deeps of diamonds, Fearnot told them of his journey. The way is long, he said, and the paths are strange. And still I have not learned to shudder. But they could not hear for glitter, they did not care for coins. No, Fearnot was a hero and that was that. They took him up and whirled him round and delight danced with them.

It wasn't until sometime later, feasting finished and all forgiven and forgotten, that Fearnot remembered his sweetheart. He ran to her house, his scarf from the shores of Arabi tucked into his shirt, his heart singing. Outside her window, he did as he had always done, and took out his fiddle. The sweet bird from Ireland flew up to the heavens and the shutters flung open. But no darling at the window. Instead, her father with a grim expression. "Come quick!" he called down. "Hurry!"

So bidden, Fearnot rushed up the stairs. The Merchant waited for him. "Where've you been?" he cried, his voice heavy with sorrow. "She swooned when she heard you'd gone, and nothing will revive her." Even as he said these things, he ushered Fearnot into his sweetheart's room. There she lay on a bed of lace, her gentle face pale, her breathing deep and distant. Fearnot's heart sank. He lay the silk

scarf across her neck while love skipped one beat and then another. He
spoke, but the words came out in a tiny whisper. "I don't know her
name," he said in a voice of despair, stroking and stroking her lovely
hair. "Lydia," said her father mournfully. "Lydia." Fearnot mouthed
the name over and over, "Lydia, Lydia," held her sweet hand in his. He
trembled with the fear she might never open her eyes, might never
smile that darling smile. But even as the little shudder shook him,
her eyelids fluttered, came open, closed, opened, closed, opened.
And she looked at her sweetheart, home at last, and smiled, and
Fearnot forgot himself and her father and kissed her cupid lips and
shivered all over.

"Oh! Will you look at that!" said Lydia's father as she sat up in her
bed. But Fearnot could look at nothing, for don't you see? Don't you
follow? Fearnot had shivered! Fearnot had shuddered! "Lydia, Lydia!
You've done it!" he cried, and kissed her again and kissed her dad and

kissed the walls and kissed the door and jumped and jumped for joy. "Done what?" asked his sweetheart dreamily. "You've taught me!" he said, brimming over with happiness. "I've been so far, so long, and all it needed was the thought of losing you to teach me what fear was." And, going to the window, he flung back the shutters, bathing the room in sunlight, and told the whole world of his triumph. "I SHUDDERED!" he told the sky. "I SHUDDERED!" he told the earth. And so the boy who set forth to learn what fear was learned it at home. And he married his sweetheart, with her name and all, and never left. And I think, though far off, Mr. McKay must have heard Fearnot's shout, for he told me all this, from start to finish, a long time ago when I was very young and didn't know the half of it.

The
Heartless
Giant

N THE whole, there's absolutely no need to be
frightened of Giants. Giants are gentle souls,
perfectly harmless, and very affectionate.
Unless, of course, the Giant has no heart
in his body.

Think of all kinds of unpleasant things and add Giant
to them and that's what you get when a Giant has no
heart. Such a Giant once terrorized a country in the far
north of the world, near the very top. He'd hidden his heart. It gave
him too much trouble, all those Giant Feelings, too much pain. In its
place was a wasps' nest. About to swarm. Put your ear to his chest and
you'd hear an angry buzzing noise.

This Heartless Giant could shake a man and shuffle his wits. He
could crack a skull with his fist like a walnut. And frequently did.
Until, at last, the old King of that country, as good as the Giant was
bad, trapped him in a giant trap and locked him in a cell. There the
Giant crouched, an inch of outside world to look at, the damp
dripping from the walls, the dull rattle of his chains, his low angry
growl a ceaseless rumble through the King's castle.

Years passed in this way until the Giant's voice had grated away to
the hoarsest whisper and folk had quite forgotten about Giants with
no hearts. And he'd be there still, in his foul pit, were it not for a little
boy whose name was Leo.

Leo was the King's youngest son. He had two brothers who were bigger. Prince Leo could leave no stone unturned, no passage unexplored, no drawer unrummaged, so incurably curious was he. One morning, scouting the far and deep of the castle, he came across a tiny, barred window set in the bottom of a huge gray wall. Looking through it, Leo saw nothing but dank dark pitch black. But as he turned away he imagined he heard something stir, and then came a growl, a low buzz of a growl. It was a frightening sound.

His brothers told him a Giant with no heart lived in this prison with the tiny window. He didn't believe them. They were older, his brothers, and forever teasing him. But next day he went back, carrying his drum. "Rat-tat-rat-ta-ta-tat," he played outside the window. From inside the dank dark pitch black he heard a rattle, like the rattle of a chain. He crept to the window and squinted into the shadows. Two eyes blinked back at him. Leo jumped. A wasp buzzed angrily through the bars. Leo ran off. It was true, there was a Giant!

All night Leo thought about the Giant, his eyes, the low rumbling growl. Next morning, he was back, "rat-tat-rat-ta-ta-tat!" on his little drum. The Giant was waiting for him. When Leo tiptoed to the window, he was there, whispering hello. The Giant told Leo that long ago he had done some bad things and that the King had locked him up. Leo couldn't imagine what these bad things were. He worried about the poor Giant, stuck down there in terrible chains. He lit a candle and held it to the hole. The Giant was so big he had to crouch with his chin on his knees and his elbows bent. He looked to Leo like a huge sad baby, his yellow eyes screwed up against the candle's sudden glare. Leo said he would speak to his father, it wasn't fair the Giant had been locked up for so long; he must have been forgotten. "No," croaked the Giant, all anxious. "If you say anything, they'll make me stay down here forever and I shall surely perish." The eyes blinked nearer. "Would you like to be my friend?"

Leo was elated. "Oh yes, yes please!" "Good. Good," said the

Giant. Good, thought Leo; I have a secret friend. Good, thought the Giant who had shed his heart; at last. And he sighed a chill sigh and planned chill plans, while the young Prince skipped back along the path, swinging the iron gate behind him, caressing his secret, nurturing it, back to his room.

And so it began, the friendship between the huge, crouching Giant and the little Prince. Every day, the boy would appear, rat-tat-tatting on his drum. Every day, he'd tell a little more, hear a little more, until he felt he knew no one better, that no one knew him better. Oh, he wanted to tell the whole world about his friend. But the Giant said, "Our secret," and Leo agreed, although he would have loved to tell his mother or his two brothers or some-body. But he couldn't so he shouldn't, so he wouldn't so he didn't. The Giant, meanwhile, crouched in his blackness and schemed. And so it was that one day he told Leo he'd heard a Guard saying that the King slept with the keys to the Giant's chains hanging on a ring by his bed. Leo had always thought those keys were for the Crown Jewels. "No," said the Giant. "They're for my misery." Leo felt desperate for his misunderstood friend, and a plan formed in his mind. The Giant watched it being born and sighed a cold sigh. Deep inside, in the place where his heart should have been, the wasps seethed and buzzed.

That very night, when the whole castle was sleeping, when the Royal Guards slumped against their sentry posts and dozed, when the owls hooted, little Prince Leo slipped from his bed, slid past a sleeping sentry, and pushed on the door of his parents' room. He tiptoed round the great bed with its velvet eiderdown, past his sleeping mother and sleeping father, to the hook where the keys were hung. They were so heavy. He heaved them up and they swung together, clanging like the Angelus bell. Leo clutched them tight, their black metal teeth squashing his toes, their looped handles framing his face. Slowly, slowly, inch by inch, he dragged the huge keys out of the room.

"I've got the keys," he whispered, trembling at the little window. He let them ring against the bars. "Who goes there?" challenged a voice from the darkness. It was the one sentry still awake. "Hurry, hurry!" growled the Giant from the bowels of the dungeon. Leo struggled to push the keys through the bars. The teeth went in and the long shafts, but when it came to the ring he couldn't work out how to do it. "They're too big," he explained as he heard the Giant's snort of impatience. "I can't do it." Leo wanted to drop the keys and run for his life. "Push them," hissed the Giant. "Push them!" The Giant's voice was colder than the night, it was icy. Leo pushed. A great hand yanked on the keys. Leo saw its shape in the shadows. He felt a terrible force pulling downward.

"Who goes there?" demanded the approaching voice. And then,

with a sudden wrench, the keys disappeared, pulling the bars with them into the blackness. Leo heard a sigh issue from the Giant. A horrible aching sigh. Then the turning of locks, the crushing of doors. "Don't forget to let me have them back," he said, staring blankly into the dungeon. He shivered again.

The sentry's torch was almost upon him. Suddenly the silence was rent with cries. A man screamed, and there was the sound of crunching, like a great walnut cracking. Then a broken, throaty roar. At the far corner, a door burst from its hinges, spilling light onto Leo's face. The Giant appeared. First his head, squeezing at the entrance, pulling away bricks and lintels, then his shoulders, squeezing, straining through. A giant baby being born into the night. Leo watched, horrified. The Giant glanced at Leo, but only for a second. As he emerged from the entrance, first one sentry, then a second confronted him, challenging him with sword and spear. The Giant hoisted them up, one in each fist, and cracked their heads together before tossing them away. Then, with the sound of groans and cries proclaiming his release, as the Guards sounded the alarm, the Heartless Giant turned and limped off, roaring his broken roar.

All night Leo sat shivering on the battlements as the King and his men searched the grounds of the castle. His father's angry words haunted him. "Someone betrayed us. Only a madman would help a Giant with no heart. Someone betrayed us." Leo's face swam with tears. So letdown, he felt. So stupid. So guilty. Every scream was his fault. Every cracked skull. And when finally morning came, the boy in him, the innocent heart, the joy in him, they were gone—those things, like his friend—and they would never return.

Next morning, Leo looked down and saw his Elder Brother march across the courtyard. He carried his sword and his axe and his bow and a large saddlebag, which he yanked up onto his shoulder. "Where are you going?" Leo called down. "Sh-h-h!" warned his brother. "I am going to get back the Giant." Leo felt awful. "Have you told anybody?" Elder Brother shook his head proudly. "No. Of course not.

But I must go. Father is too old." And with this he offered up his hand
in salute and turned, young warrior, off to find the Giant. "I'm sorry,"
wept his brother, but no one heard him.

And Elder Brother did not come back.

The spring came and went with sadness in it. Every day, more
stories reached the castle of the Giant's cruel rampage. So it was that
one glum morning, perched up on the ledge of his window, Leo
looked down and saw Middle Brother striding through the courtyard,
golden helmet blazing, shield sparkling. "Where are you going?" Leo
called out. "To find our brother and to kill the Giant." Leo was beside
himself. "Please don't! It's madness. He has no heart." Middle Brother
shook his proud head. "I must go. Our father's too old now." Leo could
not stand it. "But he'll trick you!" he blurted out. "He'll trick you!"
Middle Brother would not listen. He raised his hand in salute and

set off to find the Giant. Terrible, Leo felt, as he watched him go, terrible.

And Middle Brother did not come back either.

The summer that year was short, the winter wild and endless. One day, Leo heard his mother's sobs from far off and came into her bedroom to find her kneeling in sorrow, head against the green velvet of the eiderdown. "Mother?" The Queen did not look up. "Your father says he intends to go off and fight the Giant. I've lost two sons already. He's too old. He's too ill." She wept and wept. She wanted Leo to promise he would never follow his brothers. "Promise me, promise me you won't ever go." But he couldn't promise, how could he? Were it not for him, the Heartless Giant would still be chained and locked and safe in the dungeon.

Next morning, at the crack of dawn, dressed in a thick leather jerkin, Leo stole into the Royal Stables. He carried with him saddlebags stuffed with cheese and ham and biscuits and salted beef, but no weapon of any kind. He approached the stall where his father's stallion stood, tall, scarred, imperious, swung the saddle over the beast's back, and led him from the stable. Off they rode without looking back, their breath steaming out before them, the path flashing by, on and on and on.

And so the young Prince Leo rode the land in search of his once friend the Heartless Giant. Three winters came and went, their bitter shiver, but still he rode on, determined. And many times were the saddlebags emptied and filled; many nights slept achingly cold, huddled with his horse for warmth; many days spent without sighting a single soul. The boy changed slowly into man, took his own counsel, his jaw set in resolve, his heart firm, his plan fixed. Yet to find the Heartless Giant was no easy thing. His pillage had stripped the landscape bare. Only bleached bones, spat-out ruins, whispered nightmares remained. Where the Giant was no one knew. Long gone, the survivors told Leo as he bent from the horse's neck. Long gone.

Then one day he came to a place and knew he was finally on the Giant's trail. The sweet stench of blood curdled the air. A village, abandoned, smoldered and smoked. Leo's horse reared and bucked and was fearful. Looking down to the earth for clues, they saw a bird flap, helpless, a torn wing shuddering pitifully. The Prince set down and took up the bird in his hands. "Craa! Craa! Help me!" it cried. "The Giant broke me and now I cannot fly, cannot eat. Craa! Help me."

And Leo tended the bird, fixed its wing, fed it bread soaked in milk. And soon all was well with it. Leo threw it high into the air and watched it soar, its vivid re-ascent. "Thank you!" cried the bird from the heavens. "If you need me, I shan't forget." And with a "Craa! Craa!" it flew off. And they followed.

Not long after, Leo stopped at a brook, horse and rider hungry and thirsty, sore and weary. As they drank, they heard a flapping, heard a thrashing, heard a slapping, and, looking round, Leo saw a salmon, twisting, frantic, beached in the crook of a small crevasse. "Help me!" cried the choking fish. "Help me back into the water! I'm stuck here, I'm stranded, I'm beached up and landed! Help me!"

Now Leo was famished, and he loved salmon over the taste of any fish. But he'd suffered sufficient, this fellow, thought the Prince. He picked up the flailing fish and swung it gently into the stream, back to where the salmon is King. Off it flashed through the reeds and green ripples, before leaping up in the middle of the water, slapping the surface with its message. "Thank you!" it cried. "If you need me, I shan't forget." Then it plunged back into the brook, and they followed its zig and its zag down the stream, for that way lay the Giant.

Now neither Leo nor his horse had eaten for days. They were faint with hunger. Their progress slowed to a weary jog and stumble, until at last the old stallion sank slowly to his knees and gave up the ghost. Enough, he sighed, rolled over, and died. Leo lay beside his faithful servant and shed tears enough to break a heart, half from love, half from despair. Then he slipped into sleep. He dreamed he was in his mother's bed, warm and cherished. So warm, his mother nursing him, licking up his wet cheeks, hugging him. So vivid. He woke hugging himself, only to find a dead horse beside him and not his mother but a great Wolf coiled around his body, terrible teeth glistening, tongue hanging out with hunger.

And, seeing his eyes flicker, the Wolf howled a terrible howl, fixed on Leo's bare, unguarded throat. "Help!" howled the Wolf. "I've not eaten since the winter came. Help me and I'll not forget you." Leo had no food, save his own flesh. He took up his courage and spoke to the Wolf, whose sour breath plaited with his own, so near they were to the other's jaw. "How can I?" he replied. "I have no food myself." The Wolf nudged against the dead horse. "Then let me eat your horse," he panted, his tongue a vicious red swipe across his teeth. "I'll eat it and be strong again. Trust me. I'll help you."

The Prince could not watch as the starving animal leapt upon the flesh of the stallion. In no time, he'd eaten every scrap of flesh, chewed the bones, spat them out. Leo allowed himself a single glance from a distance. He caught the Wolf's red eyes contemplating him, the tongue sweeping the teeth, the body crouched over a mess of rib and hunk.

"Master. Come here," said the Wolf. Leo was resigned. "Am I next to go?" he asked simply. The Wolf nodded. "Oh yes, us both must go," he replied. "For you seek the Giant, I know. And now, strong again, I'll help you. On my back, sir, and let's leave this place."

Off they went a gray dash, a day and a night and a morning, until they came at last to a strange garden full of statues. Stone men. Stone women. Stone soldiers. Leo slipped from Graylegs' back and examined the statues. So lifelike were they, he felt a warmer sun might thaw them into being. He passed the bent, supplicant figure of an old woman, ivy in her stone tresses, then came to a statue of a brave young warrior, sword drawn, shield raised. Leo walked round to face it. "It's my brother!" he gasped. "This is a statue of my brother!" Graylegs the

Wolf shook his gray head. "No, my Lord, no statue. This is the Giant's work. There is his house," he continued, nodding toward a clearing. "All who approach he turns to stone."

A little way down, the Prince came across another figure, frozen in the act of straining at the longbow, arrow poised at the ear. It was Elder Brother. "You too!" cried Leo in despair. "You too."

At the end of the clearing was the place where the Giant lived, a strange building made by tearing up a whole village and squashing it into a single house. Inside, the Heartless Giant was asleep. A "rat-tat-rat-ta-ta-tat" interrupted his dreams. "Rat-tat-rat-ta-ta-tat," over and over. He heaved his huge frame to the patchwork of windows and looked out. Standing there, fearless, without weapon, beating his child's drum, was the young Prince Leo.

The Giant took Leo in as his servant. The Prince explained how it was discovered he had helped the Giant escape. The Giant laughed at this. Had he seen his brothers, stone men in the garden? Leo said he had. Any who crossed him got the same treatment, so Leo had better be on his mettle. The Giant picked up the drum between his fingers and tapped out the march rhythm, memories flooding back. "That terrible cage," he sighed. "I had to fool you to get the keys. Otherwise I'd still be there, rotting. I still limp, you know." Then he squeezed Leo affectionately in his palm. "So, my little Leo, back again. Hah! Yes, stay if you like. No tricks, though, no traps. Else you'll end up like your brothers."

"No tricks, no traps," agreed the boy and went inside.

So Leo became the servant of the Heartless Giant. For weeks he cleaned, for weeks he scoured, until spick where speck was and span where squalor. Each evening, the Giant returned from his wild outings to find the fire lit, the hearth swept, his breeches pressed. He liked this. Very nice. "Very nice," he'd say as he slurped and slopped his stew. "I should have had a servant before. I like it." He burped. "It befits a Giant." Leo bowed and cleared the plates away. He was always silent, always polite, always cleaning, always watching.

Then the Giant croaked his cracked laugh. "And I don't treat you bad, do I? For a Heartless Giant." Leo kept walking away with the dishes. He spoke without looking back, his words light and idly curious. "What happened to your heart?"

Black clouds furrowed the Giant's brow. "It's in safekeeping," he growled. Leo kept walking. The Giant continued, suddenly swelling, thumping the place where his heart should have been: "Can't feel without it, can I? Can't get hurt. Can't die from heartbreak if I haven't got one. I'm invincible!" he guffawed. Leo shrugged, impressed. "Clever," he said casually. "So where is it, then, your heart?" Wasps streamed from the Giant's mouth. "He who pries is prone to die," he warned. "Do you follow me?" "Yes." Leo walked into the kitchen. Then the Giant called after him. "But I'll tell you if you want to know. My heart's in that cupboard."

Leo was passing a huge laundry press, its old wooden doors bleached and scarred with age. He paused for an instant, felt his own heart pounding, pounding. There! pounded his heart; his heart is there! The Heartless Giant, crouching at the table, missed nothing. He smirked, belched, and slumped into an after-dinner snore.

Next morning, the Giant stalked off as early as ever. His prison years had made him fearful of walls. Out he went, all the daylight hours, roving, raging, rampaging. Leo stood at the window watching him limp and lumber away. Then he rushed to the linen press, heaved on the doors. Inside was a riot of this and that: a tusk, a trowel, a tent, a trap, a towel, a tin, a thousand trinkets. And then boxes. All manner of boxes. Leo opened them all, big or small. Two were heart-shaped. He tore at them. But there was no heart. Anything but hearts.

"I'm back," announced the Giant later that evening, tossing a brace of dead pigs on the kitchen step. The Giant sniffed into the air. A suspicious sniff. "What's that smell?" he demanded, his nose tilted up, snorting like a bellows. Leo pointed at the gleaming doors of the old cupboard. "Polish," he said. The Giant's eyes widened in disbelief. "What you polishing the cupboard for?" he demanded.

"It's the home of your heart," declared Leo. "It should be polished." The Giant roared with laughter. "Did you really think I kept my heart in a cupboard? Gah!" Leo feigned a look of disappointment, then went to the first pig and heaved it up on his shoulders to carry into the pantry. It was still warm. "If you want to know," the Giant called after him, "my heart is under the step." "Right," said Leo, treading on the stone step and continuing on his way. "That old step," chortled the Giant. "That's where my little heart beats. Ticktock."

Next morning, same story: off stomped the Giant and out went the Prince, pick and shovel, hack and hew, digging out the step, spooning out the earth. Stone. Dust. Roots. But no heart! Ach! Poor Leo. He sank down onto the step, feet in the mounds of earth, and despaired. From where he sat he could see the grim silhouettes of his brothers and their fellow sufferers. Waiting. Waiting for him to make amends.

"I'm back," called the Giant, throwing down a sack, splitting it, and revealing hares and hens and ducks and every type of small bird, all strangled. As he limped into the house, the Giant looked down to see a map of his journey recorded in huge red footprints. "What's that?" he demanded as Leo appeared. "Ah, you must have trodden on the step, sir," replied Leo politely. "I painted it." The Giant scowled. "What did you paint that old step for?" "It covers your heart, and should be special." Leo bowed. "What?" guffawed the Giant. "You're a daffle-box! You'd believe anything!" "Yes," admitted Leo. "I suppose I am, sir. I mean, I fetched you the keys to the dungeon thinking I could trust you, didn't I? So . . . yes."

The Giant didn't know how to take this. He wasn't sure whether he should feel flattered or insulted. So he sat on his chair and offered his smudged boots for Leo to remove.

"The fact is, no one can find my heart," he declared proudly. "I'll tell you exactly where it is and you'll still not find it." Leo did not look up, but continued unwinding and unwinding the bootlaces as the

Giant unleashed a torrent of directions in a single breath. "Far away, so far you could not fathom it, so high you could not climb it, is a mountain, and in the mountain is a lake and in the lake is an island and in the island is a church and in the church is a well and in the well is a duck and in the duck is an egg and in the egg . . . is my heart." The Giant poked Leo with a giant finger, bowling him over and over on the flagstones. "Not so easy, little thief, eh?" he declared. "Not such a diddle and a doddle as you thought, is it? No. Your father tricked me once. I shan't be tricked again."

That night as the Giant slept, Leo lay on his cot staring at the ceiling. An egg in a duck in a well in a church in an island in a lake in a mountain. Impossible, he decided as he stole from the house and began the journey. Impossible, he decided as he passed his brothers. Impossible, he decided as he glanced at the moon and saw, in its pale silver, his friend Graylegs the Wolf, raising his head to the wind and howling long and loud before turning and bounding toward him. In a second, they were reunited, and Leo was explaining everything. He knew, he said, he knew where the Giant's heart was, he knew how to get there, but the journey was hard, treacherous, impossible.

"Hold tight," said Graylegs, offering the Prince his back. "Hold fast." And very tight the young Prince held, and very fast, for a gray dash they went, headlong, a breathless blur of world flashing by. And they came to the mountain, clambering, scrambling. And up at last. And then the lake. Wide. Deep. "Hold tight!" the Wolf cried again. "Hold close." And plunge, splash into the lake, heads arched up above the water, cold, soaking, chilled, choking. And out at last. On the island.

In its center loomed the church, its spire so high it threatened to tear Heaven. Leo twisted the iron handles on the massive doors. The doors were locked. Nothing would budge them. Leo hammered in frustration on the thick oak panels. Above them the bells rang for the Angelus. They looked up at the swing and toll.

"Look!" cried Graylegs and, squinting into the glare, Leo saw, dangling impossibly high from the bell tower, the key. Then, mingling with the cling-clang-clang-clong-clang of the bells, came a new note. "Craa!" it sounded. "Craa! Craa!" And from nowhere the bird whose wing Leo had mended swooped past them in salute before swinging up to the tower with a single beat and pulling the key off its thread. Seconds later, the doors swung open. Sure enough, in one corner they came upon a well, and in the well swam a duck.

Leo clambered up onto the lip of the well and began to scatter bread to tempt the duck toward his open hands. He coaxed the duck with each crumb, nearer and nearer until, with a sudden lunge, he had the bird firmly in his grasp. But then, just as he pulled the duck out of the water, the egg dropped from its body back into the water, sinking into the blackness. Leo was dumbfounded. Then, miraculously, the water's skin broke and a beautiful fish leapt, twisted, turned, and plunged, then reappeared slapping the water with its tail. The salmon! Back it dived, vanished, surfaced to flip the egg high into the air. "Catch it!" howled Graylegs at Leo. And he did. He caught the Giant's heart. Held it in his hands.

For a second time, the Heartless Giant woke to the sound of a drum playing. "Rat-tat-rat-ta-ta-tat. Rat-tat-rat-ta-ta-tat." "Where've you been?" he roared in his cracked voice as he charged from the house toward Leo. "I've a good mind to set you there with your brothers." Leo ignored him, continued the little roll on his drum. "Rat-tat-rat-ta-ta-tat. Rat-tat-rat-ta-ta-tat." The Giant boiled. "Stop that!" he ordered. Leo did not stop, but spoke as he continued to beat on the drum. "Years ago, sir, you broke my heart," he said in a quiet voice. "Now I shall break yours." And with that he laid down his drum and held aloft the egg that held the Giant's heart. The Giant was terrified, paralyzed.

"No!" he whispered. "Don't . . . Be careful . . . don't break that . . . please, I beg you." Leo stood before him, the egg pressed threateningly between his palms. "I will break it," he promised. "I'll

squeeze and squeeze it to bits unless you release my brothers and all these poor people."

"Yes! Anything! Don't drop, careful, please, please be careful!" The Giant seemed to shrink with each second, his voice disintegrating to a sorry broken chord. "I'll do anything you ask," he promised, staggering toward the stone figures. "Look! I'm doing it!" And with that he limped from statue to statue, touching each one, mumbling the while. As he passed, each pose melted, softened, shuddered into life. Leo's brothers ran to him, praising Heaven, embracing him. "Brother! You've rescued us!" they cried.

The Giant limped toward the three brothers. "I've done as you bid," he whispered. "Can I have my heart?" Leo nodded. "You can, sir. As I promised. For I know that with your heart in place you could not be as you are now." The Giant sighed. "Thank you," he said, holding out his hand for the return of his heart.

Leo's brothers lunged at him, trapping his arms, snatching the egg from his grasp. Leo yelled. The Giant groaned. "Now, villain!" the brothers cried. "For five long years we've stood here helpless and watched your cruelty." Leo protested, struggled. The Giant hung his head, closed his eyes. "Please," he asked sadly. "Don't. Please." By now, the crowds of liberated souls had surrounded the group, demanding vengeance. "Kill him!" they chanted. "Kill him! Kill him! Kill him!"

"Don't!" Leo pleaded. "I promised! Don't!" But no one heard him. His Elder Brother advanced on the Giant and squeezed on the egg. The Giant staggered back, clutching the place where his heart should have been, gasping for air, short agonized gasps. The crowd roared its approval. Leo wept and wept, screaming to be heard over the cheering. His brother squeezed again. As he sank slowly to his knees, the Giant caught Leo in a terrible gaze. "You promised," he said. "You promised."

Then the egg burst in the elder Prince's hands, yolk and white slopping on him. The crowd cheered. The Giant slumped forward

and died. Wasps swarmed angrily from his mouth. Where the Giant fell a hill grew. And in time, when much was forgotten, when many Kings had come and gone, the place was still known as the Hill of the Heartless Giant.

Prince Leo lived to be a great age, became King, had forty-two grandchildren, and told them all that tale. But in his story the Giant got back his heart and made amends for all his wrongs. Because, you see, despite all that took place, a little boy once met a Giant and they became friends.

Sapsorrow

EGINNING as I do at the beginning, and starting as I must at the start, let me speak of fate in the round of a ring, let me speak of fate in the shape of a slipper. The girl whose finger fits the ring, she'll become Queen; the law decrees it. The girl whose foot fits the slipper will marry a handsome Prince. What a lucky girl, you might think.

Oh no.

A King had three daughters. Two were bad, one was good. But he loved them all alike, and what he gave to one he gave to the others. Past their perfect curls, past their painted cheeks, past their petticoats and silks, his eldest girls were sour where their sister was sweet, mean where she was gentle, hard where she was soft, cruel where she was kind. And the youngest suffered the pain of one who is below, the butt of malice. They squeezed on her bright mind until she was convinced she was simple; they taunted her fair features until she was convinced she was plain. And they gave her a name that stuck: Sapsorrow.

His wife long dead, the King's sole joy had been the joy of the proud father. Now his girls were growing up, soon there would be suitors, soon the palace would be empty. And his thoughts turned to his old age, to his loneliness. I must find a wife to comfort me, he

thought, and unlocked the little box in which he kept the wedding
ring, passed on from Queen to Queen, finger to finger, since any could
remember. Only when the ring fits can the King marry. Holding the
ring, memories ebbing from it, he made a decision. He would post the
banns, he decided. He would issue the edict.

The next morning as the dawn broke, a servant hammered a
proclamation onto the great wooden doors of the church. Then,
raising a trumpet to his lips, he blew three sharp notes of fanfare. "She
who wishes to wed our King must come forward and try the ring," he
cried, over and over, waking the city. Faces came to windows, people
came to doors, folk flocked to read the notice. And from their balcony,
overlooking the church, the Bad Sisters looked down and scowled,
furious at their father. They wanted no rival for his favor, wanted no
heir to the throne. He was too old, they told each other; he ought to be
thinking about dying soon. Sapsorrow joined them on the balcony.
She heard the proclamation and was happy for her father. Her sisters
shooed her away, disgusted, showering her with insults, calling her a
half-wit. "Go away!" they shrieked. "Ugh! Go away! Go away! Go
away!"

For when they were angry, which was often, when they were cruel,
which was always, they took out their rage on their sister. So the more
the sisters sulked at the prospect of a stepmother, the viler they were
to poor Sapsorrow. When, soon after, their father set off to find his
bride, they teased, taunted, and tormented her. They starved her.
"You're too fat," they'd say, stealing from her plate. "All this eating is
making you stupid." Oh yes, all the while the King was away they
punished her. She must polish their nails, primp their curls, wash
their feet, make their beds, however hungry she was, however sad.
They were foul, these Bad Sisters.

But Sapsorrow was friends with all the creatures of the forest, those
that crawled, those that flew; they lived in her pockets, under her
table, perched on her chair, ran through her hair. Whenever she went

to her room, she would find berries and all kinds of nuts and fruits, delicious things. For kindness repays in kindness, care in care, and the girl did not starve when the King was away.

At length he returned, the King, weary of wandering his kingdom. For the ring was a cruel shape and none could wear it, and now he despaired of any solace in his old age. As he entered the palace, the two Bad Sisters flocked to him, billing and cooing, flouncing their skirts in a gush of reunion. How sad they were, they lied; how much they'd missed him, they pretended; what a shame he'd found no bride, they clucked, delighted. And, an arm in each of his, they hugged and smothered him. "All for the best," simpered one. "Fate," tittered the other, "not intended."

Oh yes, the Bad Sisters were not past a scheme or two, not above a device when it suited. They were determined to have the kingdom to themselves when the old King died. They wanted no mother to contend with, no sister. Each day when the women came to the Great Hall to try the ring, women from far, women from wide, the Bad Sisters would sit suspiciously on their balcony, gazing down at the line, smirking as the ring failed to fit, watching anxiously in case it ever did. And though it never did, their unease grew with the lines. We should be Queens, they told themselves. We should be Queens, together. And that is why when the thought came, which one day it did, that they should try the ring themselves, it seemed such a clever one. . . . He wouldn't want to marry us if the ring were to fit, they reasoned, hugging each other, but then he couldn't marry anybody! And they congratulated themselves on their brilliance.

As the day ended, they crept down to the hall where the ring perched on its velvet pillow. One of them was rather thin, so the ring slipped off. The other was rather fat, and the ring stuck. "Ow!" she complained. "It's stuck!" Nothing would budge it. The Bad Sister's finger began to swell. It turned a purple color. "Look!" she howled. "It's turning a purple color! Do something!" But try as she might, tug as she did, the other Bad Sister could not shift it.

Sapsorrow came by and stopped, hearing the yelps and howls. Seeing her sister in pain, she went to help, and though Thin Bad Sister would have none of it, Fat Bad Sister insisted. "Let her do it!" she screamed, her finger pulsating. "She's better at these things than you are." And with gentle fingers, while Thin Bad Sister sulked and Fat Bad Sister bellowed, Sapsorrow worked at the ring until slowly, slowly, and then, with a sudden *ping,* the ring slipped off and dropped to the floor, rolling along the marble.

"What's going on?" asked the King as he hurried into the hall. "Nothing, Daddy," replied the Bad Sisters, standing in front of the empty pillow. "What was all the hue and cry?" their father said as he approached. "Hue and cry, Daddy?" asked Fat Bad, all innocence, while Thin Bad kicked Sapsorrow's shin and hissed "Pick it up!" as she jerked her head toward where the ring lay. The King, meanwhile, was confused. "There were terrible cries coming from this room," he said. "I heard them." And while Bad Sister looked to Bad Sister for an explanation, little Sapsorrow did a thing she would long regret. Obediently, she bent, and—oh folly!—she stooped and—oh rash!— she picked up the Royal ring and slipped it on for safekeeping.

Just then the King's eyes took in the empty pillow. "Where's your mother's ring?" he demanded of his daughters. The Bad Sisters, eyes fluttering, turned pointedly toward Sapsorrow. "Daughter?" pressed the King sternly. Sapsorrow shook her head, stepped back, and then, in a moment she would never forget, caught sight of the ring on her wedding finger. And what she saw the King saw too. "Oh no!" he cried in horror. Then the Bad Sisters noticed. "IT FITS!" they chorused, amazed. "It fits," whispered the King.

No sooner done, no sooner said, the news was afire in the palace, sweeping the corridors, inflaming the people. The ring fits the King's daughter! The ring fits the King's daughter! The King's daughter! The King's daughter!

And bells tolled, half in praise, half in shame. Wedding bells, funeral bells. All night, throughout the city, arguments raged. "You

143

cannot marry your father, but you cannot ignore the law. You cannot marry your father, but you cannot shame the King. You cannot marry your father, but the ring is the ring is the ring."

For three days and three nights, the King met with his council to ponder on the law, while Sapsorrow wept in her room, only her creatures for company. Finally, she was summoned to the King's chamber where her father sat, his face heavy with sorrow, his council around him, somber and resolved. Sapsorrow's heart pounded. "It is the law of the land," said the Prime Minister in a grave voice. "The ring fits your finger and you must marry the King." Sapsorrow, giddy, close to fainting on hearing what she knew she would, bit on her finger, the cold gold against her teeth, biting back the tears. "Why did you play with the ring?" asked the King bitterly. "Why did you tamper with it? Now see what befalls us." He turned to the Prime Minister. "The ceremony," he asked, "when must it take place?" And his Minister told him that the wedding must happen as soon as the preparations allowed.

Sapsorrow listened but could not hear, looked but could not see. She must escape and yet how could she? The faces of the court stared sternly at her, waiting on her response. At last, she spoke. "Then first find me a dress of the palest silk," she said, drawing herself up. "The color of the moon. I will not wed till I have it." The graybeards of the council turned to the King, who nodded. "Very well," said the Prime Minister. "We will find this dress." While men were sent out for silk, while tailors cut and needles flew, Sapsorrow stayed in her room, never appearing. For she had a scheme and shared it with the creatures. "To find such a gown will take time," she told her friends as they crawled and scurried and nested in her hair. "And meantime you must all help me."

It was not long before a knocking at the door disturbed her. The dress had arrived. There it was, pushed forward on a mannequin, the King beside it, her sisters behind, the court in attendance. "Beautiful," whispered Sapsorrow, enchanted by the pale silk, "Very like the moon." And the Prime Minister waited for her decision. "But now," she continued, her voice firm, "I must have one all in silver, sparkling with stars." The Prime Minister frowned.

"For my trousseau," said Sapsorrow.

"Sire," demanded his Minister. "Where would we find such a dress?" But the King's hopes were as desperate as his daughter's and he clung to this thread of delay. "Do as she bids," he said. "All in silver, sparkling with stars." And with that the Princess closed the door, leaving the court to ponder, her sisters to flounce off, the tailors to wander the land in search of a silver cloth that would gleam like the stars twinkling in the heavens. Little did they know that all the while, in Sapsorrow's room, another garment was being made, more marvelous and more magical. But its weaving was slow, its material rarer still than silver, and before it was done, King and court were back again.

This time, the Princess would not let them in, but stood in the doorway and looked down the corridor at the dress the Royal tailors had sewn for her. And it was like the stars. "Beautiful!" gasped Sapsorrow, entranced, for she felt as she looked at the gown as if she were gazing into the night sky. "Beautiful. Very like the stars." The Prime Minister stepped forward, anxious to proceed. "The court waits on you, sire," he told the King. "The people are impatient. When will you wed?"

The King stared sadly into the gown's constellation, searching for a way to escape such a fate, seeing none. "Daughter?" he asked, brow furrowed. Sapsorrow's huge gray eyes stared at them. "This gown is for the wedding feast," she told them. "The first one for the procession. Now I must have one for the church. Gold, it should be. Gold as the sun. Bring me that dress and the next day we shall be wed." The court greeted her answer with satisfaction, its gist whispered down the corridor, passed to the people. "Gold, she says, all gold like the sun. Bring her that dress and they will be married on the morrow."

While the tailors sewed with thread of pure gold, while the seamstresses buzzed, while the wedding feast was prepared, up in Sapsorrow's room the oil burned all night, the shutters stayed closed all day. Only her creatures were seen, flying in, slithering out, busy, busy, scurrying about. And so it was that in the same moment as the tailors delivered a dress like sunshine itself, the creatures finished their own secret task.

This time, Sapsorrow would not come out of her room to view the dress. The entourage, charged with anticipation, waited while the gown was passed behind the door for the Princess's approval. There was a silence. The Prime Minister coughed restlessly. "It is a dress such as none have seen before," he said. "Of pure gold. Dazzling. A hundred hands have sewn it."

Inside the room, Sapsorrow touched the folds of the material, brought its softness to her cheek. It was as if the sun had poured through the shutters, as if the morning had broken over her head. "It is what I asked for," she agreed, so quietly that her words were taken up by the Minister and repeated for all to hear. "It is what she asked for!" he announced triumphantly. "Yes," continued the Princess. "Very like the sun." "Very like the sun!" came the echo, and a gasp went up along the corridors of the palace. The Prime Minister turned to the assembled, his work done. "They will marry on the morrow!" he cried, and with that a hum broke out, a hubbub drowned only by bells, bells so loud that no one heard the King's sobs as the tears ran down him, weeping.

And though the night seemed to have lasted forever, the morning came too soon for the King. He dressed slowly in his furs and silks, then placed the crown on his head, and, accompanied by the Royal Guards, their uniforms sparkling, followed by his daughters, bridesmaids in flounces of pink and bows, he walked miserably to Sapsorrow's room to claim his bride. After an age of impatient knocking, the Minister ordered the door to be charged down.

Inside, the windows were open, the room was bare, and of the Princess there was no sign. A single feather floated mysteriously to the floor, landing on a small gold ring. Soldiers were sent to scour the grounds. The Princess must be somewhere, hiding in fear of the wedding. Sentries reported that no one had come or gone. Neither man nor woman had left the palace, only a strange creature of fur and feathers, scurrying along the ledges, disappearing into the bushes, swimming across the moat. One Guard noticed and thought he'd seen a large cat, another described it as a dog, a third as a seal. Sapsorrow was never found. And though the court was angry, though tongues wagged and gossips gossiped, the King's beating heart stilled, and he was happy.

Three years later and in another land altogether, a creature known as Straggletag, a poor thing of fur and feathers, tended geese in a King's garden and scrubbed the pots in his kitchen. No one knew her real name or where she came from, for she seldom spoke and then when spoken to, and was not sweet to look upon, so no one bothered with her, save as the butt of their jokes or when a job came up too dirty for one, too foul for another. She never said no and she never complained, and the geese adored her. All things that slithered, all things that flew, all things that crept from the corner adored her. She fed them the scraps of her scraps, and she slept in rags by the stove. She was a Straggletag and that was that. A Princess of Slops. A Princess of Peelings. A Princess of the Kitchen Floor. And one day this Princess met a Prince. . . .

This Prince was a handsome fellow, slender of figure, fair of feature, and very proud. He came on this day to the kitchens in search of the Cook. No one was there save the Straggletag, on her knees, polishing the flagstones. He did not approach her, but inspected the pots bubbling on the fires, for this was the day of a Royal Ball in the Prince's honor. He told the creature to give the Cook a message. He wanted goose added to the menu, roast goose with orange, baked in cider. The Straggletag glanced up, gave him a look, then nodded and continued with her work.

"What's that look?" the Prince asked sharply. The creature's voice was quiet, humble. "It's a look," she said, and polished the harder. The Prince took a few steps toward her, then demanded she explain her remark. "It's a look," she repeated, not lifting her head. "If there were a tax on looking, we'd all be beggars, sire." The proud Prince told her that it wasn't done for such as her to stare at a Prince; it was not polite in one so low or ugly. The Straggletag simply nodded, still not meeting his eyes, and polished, rubbing the stones furiously. Then, as the Prince turned on his heels to leave, she spoke again. "Why eat geese?" she asked him in a small voice. "They don't harm you." The Prince was taken aback. "Because I like geese," he said rather pompously. "So do I," returned the Straggletag, polishing, polishing. "That's why I don't eat them."

"Pass on my message," said the Prince tersely, striding up to her.

"And take that for your manners." So saying, he gave the creature a sharp kick. "Roast goose in cider," he reminded her as he departed. "A dozen."

That night they sat, the geese, twelve cold stares on the Royal table, while around them many danced, many daughters wore their mothers' pearls. And the Prince was there, handsome, admired, separate, sought after. He would dance with no one, for in that land, in that time, the dance was a song without words. The one step here, the one step there, the joined hands — these were actions that spoke of other things, of a future, each dance a small promise. So that night parents looked on and hoped. But the Prince stood and smiled but did not dance. Until late, unannounced, mysterious, a woman entered in a dazzling gown, pale silk, like the moon. The room fell quiet at her radiance. And what could he do, the Prince, but walk toward her? What could he do but lead her to the floor? And they danced. It was meant. As left to right, morning to night, dark to light, they belonged.

But when the music stopped, the beauty curtsied, smiled, and turned to leave. The Prince tried to stop her, called out as she hurried away, but to no avail. As mysteriously as she had arrived, she had gone, leaving the Prince mystified, excited, tingling, transformed. He sent out men to follow her but they could not find trace of her. The Prince wondered if he had dreamed her appearance, imagined her beauty. Then, for a moment that night, alone in his room, he thought he saw her wandering below his window; but no, it was only the moon's pale glaze sending the shadows dancing. It was only the moon.

A week later, haunted by the stranger, the Prince arranged a second Ball. Downstairs, the kitchen staff had barely recovered from the first, and the sculleries and larders were a flurry of activity. So when the Prince called down for clean towels, there was no one free to oblige him save the Straggletag, whose geese had again that day offered their

necks to the Cook's terrible twist. All fur and feathers, she crept to the
Prince's room and knocked on his door. The Prince was amazed to see
the strange creature before him and said so, shooing her away,
handling the towels gingerly, for fear they might be soiled by the
Straggletag's touch.

"Do I disgust you?" she asked sadly. "You amaze me!" cried the
Prince. Straggletag shook her head and retreated. "Look," explained

the Prince ponderously. "Cats chase mice, hens lay eggs." "And what does that mean?" the creature asked, looking at him. The Prince sighed. "It means some things have to do with other things; I have nothing to do with you. You don't disgust me, because I don't think about you." "I see," said Straggletag, and slunk away.

"I don't think about you," said the proud Prince, but if he doesn't think of her, whom does he think about? No, he can't see for the feathers, this Prince, he cannot see for the furs. That night, the second Ball, beauties came and beauties went, hopes were hoped and dances danced, but the Prince stood alone, restless, reserved, staring at the great doors of the ballroom. But nothing, no sign of his darling. Then, suddenly, a hush, then a gasp, a dividing of the room, and there she was! In a dress of sparkling silver. Like the stars in the night sky. In a moment they were dancing. There might have been no one else in the room, in the palace, in the country, in the whole world, for all they knew. Just themselves alone, these two figures, taking the same steps, sharing the same touch. Until midnight came, and again the Princess turned, fled, running from the room. "Come back!" cried the Prince, distraught. "I cannot sleep. Where do you live that I might find you?" The Princess hurried on, but called out as she ran, "I live where hens catch mice and cats lay eggs," and she disappeared into the dark, her dress dissolving into the stars on the horizon. None could follow her, none could find her. She had vanished. The poor, proud Prince searched and searched in vain, though for a second he imagined he saw her. But no, it was only the stars sparkling in the night's black velvet. It was only the stars. How his head hurt, how his tummy ached, how his heart made little somersaults.

The dawn found him mooning around on the terrace, the land stretching out before him. He had not slept, could not sleep. Sick, he felt sick, for love is a malady that only kisses will cure. "What's the matter?" It was the Straggletag, walking back from the dairy, a pail in each hand. The Prince was amazed that this creature felt able to speak to him so freely. "No one," he said, "no one else in the whole palace, in the whole kingdom, talks to me like this!" Yet even as he reprimanded her, he was glad of her company, felt comfortable in it.

The Straggletag bent her head at his harsh words, and he saw the mice running through her matted hair, shivered at her grubby rags, yet hoped she would not go. "You must forgive me," she said in her quiet voice. "You looked so sad, I wondered if I could help." The Prince shook his head sorrowfully. "You can't," he said. "Are you in love?" she asked him. "Is that it? Or are you worried that you only love your sweetheart for her beautiful gowns?"

The Prince was stung. "Were she in the humblest rags," he began. "Were she the poorest creature . . ." He faltered as visions of the beautiful Princess flashed before him. "For, you see, my darling has eyes like . . ." He thought of his darling's eyes and shrugged. "They're perfect." He saw her as he had seen her when they had danced, his arm around her waist. "She has a voice like . . ." He thought of his darling's voice and shrugged. "It's perfect." The Straggletag looked at him through her tangles, and the Prince realized it was hopeless trying to explain. "Well," he said wearily, "how can I expect you to understand?" The Straggletag sat on the steps beside him. "Then you should marry her," she whispered. "I want to!" the Prince cried, exasperated. "I want to, but I can't find her. . . ."

And so they sat, Prince and Straggletag, musing on his problem, the gardens stretching out before them, the Prince wishing it were the Princess beside him, how wonderful that would be; how strange to be confiding in this poor creature, the mice running through her hair, the animals pecking round her feet. But still they sat, and both—in their way—were peaceful.

"I have a problem like yours," began the Straggletag after a little while. "What advice would you give me?" The Prince looked at her. "Well," he said sympathetically, if rather taken aback at the thought. "I don't know your beau. What's he like?" The Straggletag's voice hardly broke above a whisper. "Handsome . . . rich . . ." She scratched at her rags as she spoke. "Really?" said the Prince, finding this hard to imagine. "And proud," continued the Straggletag. "Ah," murmured the Prince, half-listening, half-dreaming of his darling. He liked sitting with the Straggletag; if ever he found the Princess, perhaps he could clean the poor thing up, wash her hair, and make her his sweetheart's servant. "But, you see," said the creature, starting him from his reverie, "when I think about him, it makes my head hurt and my tummy ache and my skin tingle and my heart do little somersaults."

"Me too! Me too!" cried the Prince. "Oh yes! We're in love and it's terrible." The Straggletag was thrown. "I don't think I'm in love," she said. "Yes," insisted the Prince. "You're definitely in love. Little somersaults? Tingling skin? Definitely." "Oh," said the Straggletag, and so they sat, together and alone, alone and together, until their peace was shattered by an angry voice. "Straggletag! Straggletag! Where the devil have you got to?" It was the Cook, full of impatience. The Straggletag stood and heaved up the pails. The Prince watched her go. "Listen," he said, embarrassed. "Don't tell anyone we've spoken." How this wounded the creature. "As you wish," she whispered. The Prince felt guilty and tried to explain. "It's just, you know, Prince and—" He couldn't think of a polite word. "Straggletag!" bellowed the Cook, completing his sentence for him. Prince and Straggletag . . .

Oh yes, the Prince is lovesick all right. And love, as we know, can't see what's in front of its nose. No, he's smitten. Even before dark, he was ready, tense and distracted on the terrace in front of the ballroom, for there was to be a third Ball that very evening. Tonight, he thought, shivering, I'll see my love tonight. And while he waited, holding his breath for sight of his darling, down below in the steaming kitchen, as full dishes poured out and empty plates poured in, the Straggletag worked, scrubbing, soaking, cleaning, hurrying, desperate to finish. All around her the servants chattered. "She hasn't come," said one. "He's there, poor love," said another. "He hasn't even gone inside." The Straggletag doused the dishes anxiously. "Can I have them, please!" she demanded of the servant who lounged at the sink, clutching a tray loaded with dirty plates. "What's the hurry?" quizzed the servant. "Meeting a sweetheart?" "Maybe," whispered the Straggletag. This sent the servant into convulsions of amusement. "That's why the Prince is still waiting!" he explained to the others, "She hasn't finished the dishes!" And they all laughed.

Upstairs, the dance was nearly over. Guests left, passing the Prince, who had not once moved from his place on the steps. He searched the heavens for his darling. Over and over, his heart flipped until he was dizzy with longing. But of the Princess there was no sign. And then, at last, from looking at the moon, from looking at the stars, he saw something impossible, for surely coming slowly up the steps toward him was the sun itself. It was her! She had come! His sweetheart, dressed in a golden gown that shone like the sun, that shimmered. The Prince swept her up and they danced, there on the terrace, with the music distant, winding into their steps. And it was wonderful.

But bells toll. Evenings end. As the clocks chimed the midnight, the Princess turned and hurried off. "Don't go!" cried the abject Prince. "Don't leave me again." But she did go, she had to. She ran off, stumbling for a second on the steps, eluding his clutching arms, running off under veil of dark, disappearing again, a glimpse of gold here, a glint there, then gone, gone, as if the sun had set and the night had come. The Prince watched, hopeless, distracted, then looked down at the terrace. At his feet was a golden slipper. He picked it up and held it to his trembling heart.

At first light, a notice was proclaimed throughout the kingdom. "The Prince will marry the girl whose foot will fit the golden slipper."

And so they came, the would-be brides, in droves, one shoe off, one shoe on, to try their luck with the slipper. The ballroom was emptied, and the moonstruck Prince sat at one end and watched them come and go at the other, knowing before the anxious squeeze or the hopeless

155

slip that this wasn't the one, waiting the while for the hush that would signal the entrance of his love. So he sat while the women came and went, for what seemed an age.

Belowstairs, the servants gossiped and predicted. "It fits nobody," said one to the next. "It's not a normal slipper, you'd think they'd realize," said another. "I might try," said a third. The others scoffed, "You've got feet like Yorkshire puddings!" they teased. All the while, the Straggletag worked, cleaning here, scrubbing there, listening. "What about our little beauty?" asked the Yorkshire Pudding, prodding her. "Will you try?" The Straggletag kept her head down. "I might," she whispered. Gales of laughter from the servants. "She might!" they howled.

And so up she went, up the stairs, into the Great Hall where the women lined up waiting their turn, and would you believe it, whom did she see pressing her foot into the slipper? None other than a big Bad Sister! The Straggletag hung back in the shadows, watching in disbelief as first one sister tried on the slipper and found it too loose, then the second, who seemed, with a huff and a puff and a tremendous effort, to prize her foot into the shoe. The Prince, hardly watching, was slumped in his chair. Suddenly the Fat Bad Sister shouted and he sat up with a start. "I've done it!" she cried. "IT FITS!" And sure enough, there she was, the golden slipper snug on her foot. The Prince was dumbfounded. "Impossible!" he barked. "You're not the one!" "I am!" insisted the Bad Sister, showing him her foot. "I most certainly am!" And with that she turned to the assembled and proclaimed in her loud foghorn: "I claim this handsome Prince for my husband."

A Page stepped forward and sounded the trumpet. "According to the proclamation," he began in a somber voice, "the Prince must marry the woman who can wear the golden slipper. That woman has now come forward." "Princess Badsister," announced Princess Badsister, identifying herself. "From?" asked the Page. "From Faraway," she told him. "From Faraway," intoned the Page before hesitating again and inquiring, "Daughter of?" "Daughter of nobody!" whispered the Bad Sister crossly, and then, to the Prince, "We have no parents," she simpered. "Mummy died a long time ago and Daddy died last year." The Prince nodded blankly. "He was ancient," added the Bad Sister. In the commotion, no one heard the gasp from the shadows, no one saw the tears well up in the Straggletag's eyes, tears of sorrow, tears of relief.

The Page began again: "Princess Badsister, from Faraway, daughter of nobody. She will marry the Prince on the morrow!" "Hurray!" exclaimed the Bad Sister, and hugged the Prince. Then she hopped a little, grimaced, and grinned all at once. "Now," she said, her smile thinning, "can I take this silly shoe off?" The Prince, hitherto silent, looked up. "Why?" he asked. "Because it's a teensy-weensy bit tight." The Bad Sister smiled, hopping a little more. "Just a pinch." Her mouth started quivering. "Ouch," she whimpered. "Because actually I think it's just an itsy-bitsy stopping the blood going round—ouch! ouchy-wouchy! In fact, I may have to have a baby scream!" And with that the tiniest scream issued from her twitching lips. The smile became increasingly extravagant, and she began to hop furiously in a curious private waltz. She took a sharp breath and hopped over to her sister. "Could you just help me, do you think?" she muttered frantically. "Just to pull this lovely slipper off my footsie-wootsie? Because I am going to have to scream very loudly shortly. I think my leg is turning a little bit on the maroon side." She turned to the Prince and gave him her biggest smile yet, an enormous grin. Then she took in a huge lungful of air. "Aaaaaarghhh!" she screamed. "GET THIS SHOE OFF MY FOOT!"

Now Prince, her sister, the Page, the rest of the court, anyone and everyone surrounded the writhing Princess Badsister and wrestled with the offending slipper. Amidst howls and moans and screams and groans, the shoe suddenly flew into the air and dropped, fate its map, at the foot of the Straggletag, who bent, picked it up, and walked toward the melee.

"I claim my right to try the slipper," she said in her quiet whisper. "Ladies, I think—not creatures!" hissed the Bad Sisters, disgusted at this thing scurrying toward them. "May I?" asked the Straggletag, looking levelly at the Prince. "Very well," he said, shrugging, indifferent now to anything and everything. "Ugh!" chorused the Bad Sisters, shuffling away from the Straggletag. "Get rid of it!" But the Prince nodded to the creature to go ahead, and she bent to the floor and, in a single gesture, slid the slipper easily on to her foot. The Bad Sisters were flabbergasted. "It fits!" they cried. "It can't do!" "It does fit," said the Straggletag softly. "Will you keep your promise?"

The room fell silent. No one moved. Eyes traveled incredulously from the tangled straggle of hair to the gleaming slipper. The Prince swallowed, shook his head, swallowed again, his world in pieces. "Very well," he muttered forlornly. "I will marry you. I will keep my promise." A murmur filled the room, a buzzing, a swell of outrage. Then suddenly, magically, from every quarter, from every nook and cranny, creatures appeared, things that scurried, things that flew, hurrying, flying toward the Straggletag, engulfing her in a cloud of whirring, beating activity. While all looked on, bewildered, an extraordinary transformation took place. For before their very eyes, the hapless, pathetic creature became a beautiful woman, standing radiant in a dress shimmering with gold, as if the sun had burst into the Great Hall.

"Sapsorrow!" exclaimed her two Bad Sisters. "You!" cried the Prince. "My Princess! It's you!" And of course it was Sapsorrow, and of course it was his Princess. She walked toward her sweetheart and they embraced, and for all they knew the world had gone away and left only their tummies to ache, their skin to tingle, and their hearts to leap over and over and over together. "Darling, darling," they repeated to each other. "Dearest, dearest." And what the Prince didn't know he very soon did. They talked and talked, explaining this, explaining that: stories of rings, stories of fur and feathers. And they wept for her dear father whose death had freed her, smiled for poor Straggletag, forgave the Bad Sisters, and danced for a day without going away. And after all that, they were so out of breath they lay down and slept . . . and glory be: if they don't wake soon, they'll never get wed!

A Story
Short

ESTERDAY I was telling a marvelous tale of how the
moon became round, and suddenly, as I reached the
best bit, I couldn't remember what came next. I
still can't. Staring at the expectant faces, I thought,
What will I do when there are no more stories
in me? When the well runs dry? What use a
Storyteller without stories?

Yesterday I forgot a story, and that is why
I went straight out and gave my supper to a
Beggar. Now, of course, this will strike fools as foolish and Wise
Men as wise. A fool eats his last potato. A Wise Man plants it.
Apart from which, everyone knows Beggars are never what they
seem. There was a time when I myself was forced to beg. A bad
time, a cold time, when a great hunger was on the land and only
the rich had bellies. And so it was that one morning I found myself
in sight of a palace and in smell of a kitchen, drawn there by the
sweet sweet aroma of roasting. I came to a door and stood decipher-
ing each strand of scent . . . duck, goose, lamb. Mmmmm. And
just about to knock was I when a raggedy character came flying
through the air, launched by the boot of a round red Cook.

"Out!" bellowed the Cook to the bewildered Beggar. "And stay out
of my kitchen!" Then his hot face swiveled and noticed me, no Prince
myself, in my torn green cloak of patches and my cheeks sucked in

with hunger. Before he could bring his boot to my own threadbare pants, I introduced myself with a flourish. "I have boiled men for wasting my time" was the Cook's inhospitable reply. I thought on this and then remarked on the wisdom of such a measure. I did not want to waste his time, I told him humbly. I simply wanted a little water to make myself some soup. And with that I scratched a stone free from the ground and held it up. Stone soup, I explained, polishing it on my cloak.

The Cook puffed out his cheeks. "You can't make soup out of a stone," he scoffed. "Oh yes I can," I said, smiling, and winked at the poor Beggar on the ground beside me. Then, bowing and scraping, I plunged into the steamy delights of the kitchen, the Beggar slipping in with me, and while the Cook filled a large pot with cold water, I beamed to the old Beggar. "Master Cook is a fool," I whispered. "He cuts the meat and others eat," and we watched as the pot of water was placed over the scorching flames. "Now!" boomed the Cook, his face shining like an apple, his head wobbling pompously. "Let's see this stone soup."

With great ceremony, I dropped the stone into the water and put my ear to it, listening carefully, the Cook watching my every move with a suspicious glare. Then, satisfied, I straightened up and folded my arms. "How long is this going to take?" demanded the Cook. "Not long," I assured him. "About an hour." With that, I stuck a finger into the pot and sucked on the liquid. "Marvelous water," I pronounced it. And so it was that our friend the Cook stood over me for an hour as the soup boiled, while one by one all the kitchen boys gathered around us to see this marvelous recipe, a simple stone in bubbling water.

"Well?" the Cook bellowed as the hour was up. I stirred the water with a ladle and sipped. "Mmmmmmmm," I murmured, wearing my best smile, and "Oh yes!" The Cook wanted a taste. "Do you have a little salt?" I inquired politely. "Salt!" roared the Cook to his minions, who scattered, then returned with a dish. In went the salt, in went my

ladle. "Mmmmmmmmm!" I reported, licking my lips. "Almost perfect." Then I allowed the smallest flicker of misgiving to cross my eyes, sharing my doubts, one cook to the other, as he waited for a sip. "Is there any stock? The tiniest drop?" "Stock!" and the minions were off again, and back with the juices in a jiff. And after stock I needed greens, and after greens I needed potatoes, then a carrot, then an onion. In they all went, stirred round, bubbling up, my eyes darting from pot to Cook, then from Cook to the Beggar, who looked on, his wise eyes twinkling with merriment. Finally came lamb, beef, a platter of best meat. The Cook shoveled it in, until I stopped him

162

with a warning hand. "Careful!" I said gravely. "You'll drown the soup," and ate the last piece to prevent him from doing so. The stone soup was ready.

I carried the pot to the table and ladled out three bowls, the whole kitchen following behind me. We sat, Cook, Beggar, your man, and drank it down. "Good," pronounced the Cook, "very good!" and had a second bowl, then a third, the Beggar and I matching him spoon for spoon. "Stone soup!" he muttered between each gulp, his head shaking in disbelief. "Marvelous." And the minions applauded, hoping for a taste. Full to the brim, I wiped my mouth, then fetched the scalding stone out of the pot with the ladle. "Keep this," I said, all generous, and lobbed it into the Cook's greedy fat fingers. He caught it eagerly and sat, happy, a man with a magic stone, until the treasure began to sizzle in his hands. "Owwwwwwwwwww!" he screamed and fell back, spilling soup, stone, plate and all, landing in a furious rage on the floor. "Owwwwwwwwwww!"

Moments later, I found myself in a sorry state, thrown to the ground in front of the court while the beetroot Cook, hand smarting, temper erupting in spits of bile, recounted my mischief to the King. A man with a full stomach can bear a great deal. I wasn't listening to them. I was listening to the sweet gurgles of my digestion. Let them rant and rave, I thought. I was working up a fine belch. For all I knew, the Cook would burst soon with his fury and that would be the end of it.

Meanwhile, he seemed to be stressing each point of his tale with a sharp kick to my ribs, not very nice. Enough, I thought, and then realized someone was speaking to me. "Answer the King, blockhead!" bellowed the Cook. Oh dear. I looked up and saw His Majesty waiting on a reply to a question I hadn't heard. Next to him sat the Queen, her long neck twisted in a question mark, and in front of their throne the Prince, a boy with the eyes of an imp, who carried a small stuffed toy in the shape of a teddy bear, whose head he twisted, staring at me. "Yes," I answered tentatively, hoping that might do. "What is your trade, fool?" demanded the Cook, with another swipe at my sore ribs. "It can be scratched on your gravestone." I didn't much like the sound of this.

"I am a teller of stories," I began, my eyes fixed on the head of the teddy bear as it twisted and twisted. "A weaver of dreams. I can dance, sing, and in the right weather stand on my head. I know seven words of Latin. I have a little magic and a trick or two. I know the proper way to meet a dragon, can fight dirty but not fair, and once swallowed thirty oysters in a minute. I am not domestic. I am a luxury, and in that sense, necessary."

There was a silence as the Cook looked to the King, who looked to the court, who looked at me, who looked at the King. The teddy bear's head turned full circle in the Prince's grip, the Queen's neck swung elegantly round, and the Cook glared, waiting for my sentence. Suddenly a laugh broke the hush, a gurgle, then a gush, then a full-throated cackle. It was the King. "Excellent!" he guffawed, delighted. "And you can make soup out of a stone! Excellent. And a monkey out of a Cook!" He laughed, and so, of course, the court laughed. Everybody laughed, including me, except the Cook, whose pink face went red, then puce, then purple, then maroon. "But, Your Majesty," he began in dismay. The King ignored him. "And stories, eh?" he continued, all interest. "Good stories? Funny stories?" I shrugged. "Some good, some funny." Then proudly, "Some indifferent."

The Cook was seething. Why was the King asking me about stories when he should have been talking about eye-gougers, racks, instruments of torture, or, better still, the boiling oil?

"Your Majesty," he wheedled, "the punishment!" The King looked at him vaguely. "Punishment." He frowned, and my heart caught in my mouth. "Yes," he decided, his voice solemn. "For your punishment, you must tell me a story every night for a year. And for each story I will give you a golden crown. Is that fair?" A golden crown! I wanted to dance, wanted to kiss him, wanted to yelp with glee. "It's my usual fee," I replied without blinking an eyelid. A golden crown! "Good." The King smiled, the court smiled, your man smiled.

Then he began again, and the smile slid slowly from my face and sizzled on the floor. "Of course," he said, "if you run out of stories for any reason, or repeat yourself—if there's one thing I hate, it's hearing the same story twice—if that were to happen, naturally I'd hand you over to the Cook and his boiling oil. Naturally." I swallowed. The Cook cackled. "Naturally," I said, gulping. The Prince, all innocent face and bubbly curls, giggled and pulled the head off his toy, looking at me.

But oh the balmy days that followed! The plenty! Much of this and much of that. Each day an inch on my belly and a story from my head. Imagine me then: a Royal commission, a servant, a feather bed, a suit of silk jingling with my gold pieces. Blissfulness. After supper, up by the fire, I would tell my tale to the rapt King. And he never fell asleep. What more could an artist want? Food to eat, money to spend, and his audience awake . . . each night a tick on the golden calendar and a snuggle with my new wife. Oh, that wife . . . Aye-ya. And how quickly the months came and went, shaking my hand, clapping my back. But there, even on my loftiest perch, I was still on my own behind. . . .

The year passed, the final day came . . . my last of sweet punishment, my wife all softness in our bed, the coins brimming over. And I woke up, full to the brim with life, and blow me—I couldn't think of a story! My mind raced through the store, but no, I'd told that one and that one and that one, and all I could think of was oil boiling. In a twink, I was up and pacing the gardens, that old crocodile, fear, leading me a merry dance. And it led me, sick to the soul, to the grate above the steaming kitchens where, looking down, I could see the pot bubbling, bubbling, bubbling. My mind was a terrible blank. Oil, it whispered; the oil is on the boil.

Slowly, sorrowfully, I trudged back to my terrace to seek solace in the sweet arms of my sweetheart. She was there, at the gate, waiting for me, her darling eyes smiling. I bowed my head mournfully. When I looked up, the Beggar was beside her, just as I had seen him a year before, rag and straggle, a Mr. Mischievous. A gold tooth, a white tooth, a yellow tooth, a gap tooth, all grinning at me. A black boot and a brown slipper and a coat of all the coats that ever were thrown away. In short, a fine fellow-me-lad of the road, with a smell to match.

Now I remembered him, as indeed who would not, but this was no time to relish the stone soup or savor old victories. I gave him a sharp smile and a short nod and offered him a piece of gold to be about his business. He didn't want my money, he said, and produced a leather purse that clinked. Inside, he said, were three hundred and sixty-four gold pieces, the same number that jingled in the chamber pot beneath our bed, the same terrible number that marked the days of my bliss, one short of a year, one foul of fortune, one less than freedom, one fewer than I needed of tales to keep me from the oil's fierce embrace. While I dwelt on the bitter nearly of the number, he opened up his purse and poured the pieces, every one, into a neat, shimmering pile at my feet. He would wager them, he announced, against my own.

Oh no, not then, though I was partial to a bet. Not then, though I was greedy for the gold. I turned away. But my wife whispered her beguiling whisper, "I warned him you were a devil with the dice," and hugged me, pulling me back to the pile. "Well, I am," I agreed. "But I can't be gambling for money. I am playing for higher stakes. I must find another story before nightfall, else I am boiled in the oil." My wife seemed unconcerned. She ran her fingers through the coins. "Oh, play," she urged. "Play." Her smile was as sweet as a honeysuckle. "You must surely win. . . ."

I know. I shouldn't have. But the gold sparkled. I should have said no. But the gold glittered. Out came the dice and we settled down to

play, the two of us kneeling to the game, my wife clapping her hands to each shake of the cup. Within an hour, my fortune sat with the Beggar's, my last coin gone, the morning wasted, all lost, all squandered. "Well, that's it," I sighed. "I have no story and no money."

The Beggar smiled his row-of-teeth smile. "Play on?" he asked, eyes twinkling under the mess of eyebrow. "With what?" I said, pointing at my empty pot, his groaning pile. The Beggar laid his hand on my darling. "Your wife," he suggested, shrugging. "Your wife against my winnings." I would not, and said so. "Never!" I declared. But my wife clapped her hands excitedly. "Yes!" she cried. "Go on! Play! I'm sure you'll win." But the thought of losing her was unbearable. "I'll not. I'll not give you up," I insisted. "I may forget stories, I may lose my fortune, I may boil, but I'll not lose you." Again came the squeeze on the arm, followed by the tenderest of kisses. The last she ever gave me. The thought of her voice still grieves me. "Play," she said. "I know you'll win."

I didn't want to. I didn't want to. The dice felt cold in my palm. I rolled them along the flagstones. Two sour dots. Two. I had lost. I had lost my darling.

My wife let go of me and hurried across to the Beggar, taking him in her arms, kissing and cuddling him with great relish. My poor heart heaved. "What's this?" I cried. My wife looked up from her billing and cooing. "The Beggar is now my husband," she told me, her lips, her lovely lips, planting sweetness on the Beggar's grizzled cheeks, "and I needs must love him." I was ready to plunge into the oil.

The Beggar picked up the dice. "Again?" he inquired, beaming. "With what?" I whispered. "There is nothing more." The Beggar offered his wager. "I'll stake everything," he offered, "wife, winnings, everything, against your own self." He picked up the dice. "Third time lucky," he suggested, all friendship and encouragement. "Stake my own self?" I replied. "Why not? You have it already anyway." The bargain struck, he rolled the dice, which hurried along the stones, rushing to their triumphant display. Two sixes . . . "Two sixes!" trilled my wife, delighted, hugging the Beggar, from whom lice fell and fleas flew.

"Two sixes." I observed, my heart empty, my head aching. "Well, sir, I am your servant on this dismal day." The Beggar nodded and produced from nowhere a long length of rope looped in an ominous noose, which he slipped over my head. "Am I to be tied up like a dog?" I cried, dismal, dazed, and despondent. "No, my friend," sniggered the Beggar. "Like a hare." And with that he pulled tight on the noose. Something happened. I shrank. I shriveled. I shook. I shuddered. Whiskers sprouted, ears flopped, my hands curled into tiny paws. I jumped, my legs jackknifing, and a terrible squeal came out of my mouth. I was transformed into a hare!

The terror of my torment! Dogs appeared, great, fat, hungry hounds, their lips slavering, their teeth snapping, their barks booming. I ran—no, I fled; no, I flew—streaking off into the gardens, the dogs baying in pursuit, my wife's cruel cackles ringing in my ears. "Help!" I cried. "Help! Help!" I dashed headlong in my new body. "Help me!" But no words came out, only a squeal, a squeal only. The dogs closed, panting, nearer and nearer, closing for the kill. The gardens I had strolled daily, preparing my stories, were suddenly a deadly course of hidden chasms and unexpected mountains, of thorns and nettles and obstacles. My four tiny legs carried me for all their worth, bobbing away from the brutal teeth. I had no breath, I had no breath . . . I was done for!

I had circled back onto the terrace, and with a final leap I launched myself into my wife's arms just as a snapping jaw tore at my fur. Next minute, she held me by my ears and dangled me over the hounds, swinging me to and fro, my wife did this to me, lowering me inch by inch, each swing a whisker nearer to the hot breath of the hounds, she

laughing, me squealing. Horrible! Horrible! "Do you like our games?" she chirped. "No, I don't!" I squealed. "Help me!" But they couldn't hear me. "Loving every minute!" the Beggar decided on my behalf. "Good, because I have better sport in store." He picked me up, poor shivering hare, and slipped the noose back round my throat. "But not in that shape," he muttered, pondering my fate. "I wonder . . ." "Don't wonder!" I squealed help- lessly. "Help me!"

But the Beggar paid no attention to my pleas. He was too busy relishing my wife. "You choose, madam," he said, stroking her beautiful red hair. "Can you do anything?" she asked, believing he could. And he nodded. "Anything," he affirmed. "But it must be small for my purposes." I hung, a hare, swinging over the hounds while my wife considered my destiny. "A flea?" she asked, wondering. The Beggar showed her his white, gold, yellow, and gap. "A flea," he said, "is possible." No sooner said, no sooner done. The Beggar tugged on the rope until I thought I must surely choke. My heart pounded, my head ached, and then I was there — or, rather, wasn't there. I looked down at myself — a tiny, dancing speck of a flea, lost in the folds of the Beggar's cloak. A flea . . . nice, I could be popped between the fingers. If you itch, think of me.

The Beggar turned and blew a kiss to my darling. "It's best you stay here, madam." he told her. "We shall return." And without more ado he strode off. Where he carried me, I knew not. This morning a man blessed; by midday a flea. It did not bode well for the evening.

You get a view on life as a flea. The human body is a hot home for the poor parasite: to drink the goblet of sweat, to nibble dirt, to weed the armpit — this is our lot. On my friend the Beggar, I was in good company. He took us all to the kitchens, and for a terrible moment I feared the worst, saw my wretched life sizzling away in the pot. He knocked purposefully at the door, and out came the Cook, all greased and lathered. My companions flew off to a feast. I stayed where I was, preferring the devil I knew. The Cook knew nothing, though he itched; saw nothing, though he scratched. No, my dears, all he noticed was the gold, spilled out onto his chopping board. The Beggar had a wager for him. Gold was the bait. The Cook bit.

The Beggar laid three straws in front of him. The Cook watched carefully. "Now," he began, "you say you can blow away two of these straws and leave the middle one where it is?" "My gold says I can," challenged the Beggar. "A meal says I can't." The minions gathered to watch this, the Cook leering at them, relishing the coins, furiously counting them. "Go on, then!" he cried eagerly, rubbing his fat hands together.

The Beggar smiled and bent forward, placing a finger on the outer straws and blowing on the middle one. It shot off the table. "That's cheating!" roared the indignant Cook. "That's cheating! I could do that!" The Beggar shrugged, throwing me across his shoulders. "Try," he told the Cook. "Go ahead." The Cook, snarling, deceived, replaced the middle straw and did as the Beggar had done, planting a finger on the outer straws and blowing hard at the middle one. And, indeed, the middle straw flew off, landing in the bubbling pot of oil. Trouble was, my dears, so did his two fingers, flying in and disappearing with a terrible sizzle.

"My fingers!" screamed the unhappy Cook, staring at his hand and counting, one, two, three . . . one, two, three. The Beggar beamed. "Not so easy," he said cheerfully. "Another game?" The Cook was in shock. "My fingers, my fingers!" he moaned, hopping distractedly from foot to foot, his lip jutting out far enough for a baby to sit on. "This is simpler," the Beggar tempted. "I wager all my gold that I can move one ear but not the other." "That's impossible," muttered the Cook, clutching his unfortunate hand. "But I'll not bet." Tears dripped down his red cheeks.

"Fetch a doctor!" he bellowed at his boys. "Fetch needle and thread. My poor fingers!" The Beggar began scooping the gold coins back into his purse. "As you wish," he said, jingling the pieces. The Cook could not bear to see them go. How could the Beggar move one ear without the other? It was impossible. He was losing the gold for no reason. It was unfair.

"No, try," he blurted out. "I want that gold. Try, and curse you." The boys held their breath, the Cook loomed over the Beggar, the Beggar put his hand to his ear and wiggled it. The Cook was outraged. "That's cheating!" he roared to the onlookers. "He's cheating." The Beggar disagreed. "No," he said. "I said I'd move one ear and not the other, and that is what I've done." The Cook wiped his three-fingered hand across his mouth, a snarl replacing it. "You'll not make a fool out of me," he warned. "I'll do it myself." And, so saying, he yanked on his ear and pulled it clean away. There it was, pink and perfect, not by his cheek where it lived, but in his hand, where it didn't.

"My ear! My ear!" he howled, hopping around the kitchen, beside himself. "Oh no! My fingers! My ear!" Then he erupted, his rage terrible, his roar trumpeting. "I'll kill you! I'll kill you for this!" And he would have had not the Beggar disappeared, his gold with him, your man clinging on for dear life. "Where's he gone?" demanded the Cook, carving the air with a cleaver. "Where's he gone?"

Where indeed? I do not know and cannot tell. The day passed in a turmoil and a whirl and a wind, more wonders than I can remember, more frights than I can forget. And then, as night drew up its hood and the appointed hour came when the King would want his story, I found myself carried to the court on the coat of the Beggar. Inside, the King grew impatient for my appearance. A servant stepped forward to inform him of the Beggar's arrival. "Sire," he said, "there is a man outside who would entertain you." Short shrift the King had for his message. "I don't want an entertainer!" His Majesty barked.

"I loathe entertainers! I want my story and I want it now!"

The Beggar would not be discouraged. He heard all this, waiting in the shadows, but stepped forward unabashed. "Majesty," he said, bowing, "allow me to present myself, ragbag that I am." The King's son, sniffing, complained noisily, "He smells!" The Beggar smiled. "I am a Beggar, sir," he explained. "It is my business to smell. But I am capable of much. I am capable of offense not simply to the nose. And I can throw a rope in a special way." Once again, from nowhere, the magic rope appeared, and with a single flourish the Beggar threw it into the air, where it hung as if held from above by an invisible hand, its tail resting on the King's great table.

"That's clever," said the King, suddenly interested. The Prince was excited. "Do something else!" he demanded before turning to the King: "Can he do anything else?" "I can," said the Beggar, and indeed he could. From the folds of his cloak, he produced a round turquoise ball, which hummed and shimmered and glowed, spinning in his palm. As the court watched, enchanted by the ball's drone and turn, the Beggar removed his hand and the ball floated gently to the ceiling, where it promptly disappeared.

"Where's it gone?" said the Prince. "I want it. Where's it gone?" The Beggar shrugged his shrug and smiled. Now the Queen intervened, her swan's neck craning forward. "The Prince wants the ball," she told the Beggar curtly. "Please oblige." The Beggar opened his hands innocently. "It's at the top of the rope," he said, as if that were sufficient reply. The Prince leapt onto the table, squinting into the dark of the ceiling. "Can I get it?" he pleaded. But his mother refused, "He can't climb a rope," and his father agreed, "You'll fall." Ever helpful, the Beggar stepped forward, grasping the rope and pulling apart the strands, the hemp teased out into steps, so that now, when the dumbfounded court looked, they saw a ladder pointing up to the roof. Without further ado, the Prince clambered up, higher and higher into the shadows. Every head in the room twisted up to watch

the Prince's progress. Up and up he climbed until they could no longer see him. There was a long silent pause. Then, with an ominous slap, the rope tumbled to the floor. I winced, if fleas can wince, and waited for the crash that must surely follow as the Prince came plunging after it, but it never came. The Prince had vanished. Then, with a spin and a hum, the turquoise ball reappeared, sailing down. All eyes followed it as it landed and bounced. Once, twice, three times. The room hushed. Silence. Then a babble of muttering and whispering, pointing, glares and indignation, all aimed at the smiling Beggar, all drowned by the terrifying roar of the King: "TO THE OIL!"

And with that Guards threw themselves on the Beggar and carried him aloft to the kitchens, a mad procession bayed on by the crowd, the Queen screaming rage, the King bellowing, "To the oil! To the oil!" I was there in the thick of it, buried in the Beggar's undergrowth. I shouted for help, but no noise came out. How many fleas screaming for rescue have we so ignored? How many ants have tried to warn us before the foot comes down with its crushing squelch? Look out! Look out! But we don't see them. They didn't see me. No, headlong we hurtled, the dark passages of the palace, the winding stairs, helter-skelter to the oil.

In we flooded, knocking pots and pans before us, to where the Cook stood, working up a fine froth, purple, panting for revenge. I couldn't watch. I couldn't speak. To go like that—a flea, a nothing. To sizzle. Horrible. I closed my tiny eyes as the Cook ranted. "Oh yes, Mr. Ragtag, here we are!" he welcomed as the Beggar was carried toward where the oil simmered. "Come to the pot, so terrible hot, come for a boil in the boiling oil!" And, with a terrifying chorus, they lifted us, Beggar and Storyteller, lifted us above the cauldron. "IN!" they roared, "IN!" they chanted, and flung us pell-mell and without so much as a by-your-leave, tossed us into the smoking pot, flung us into the scalding oil. . . .

Nothing happened. I held my breath, I said my prayers, I mouthed my goodbyes to the mortal coil, but nothing happened. The oil was as cool as a fine shower in the summer. We went down, then came up, the Beggar whistling, washing himself in the bubbles. The court gaped, the Cook blustered. "That's not right," he muttered, frowning at the King. "That's not meant to happen, sire. It's boiling." Poor Cook. "It's boiling, you see," he explained to the bewildered crowd, who stared, dazed, amazed, and confounded as the Beggar washed and whistled.

Even as he spoke, the Cook stuck in a hand to test the temperature. There was a horrible rush of bubbles to the place where his hand had plunged, a billow of smoke, a foul sizzle, and a curdling scream from the Cook as he pulled out his hand in agony. "Ooowwwwww!" he screamed, weeping pitifully, clutching his fingers. Gingerly, his brow furrowed, he uncurled his fist to inspect the damage. Then he realized . . . he blinked, his mouth puckered, he began to count in a whisper, one, two, three, four, five!

"They're back!" he cried, flexing his hand, holding it up to the crowd. "My fingers! They're back!" Hardly daring to hope, he put his hand to the place where his ear had been, and felt. It was there! "My ear!" he said, tears of joy coursing down. "It's here! My ear is here!" And he danced a dance of pure joy, tugging on his fingers, tugging on his ear, a man restored.

The others, King and Queen, confused and astounded, looked from ecstatic Cook to steaming pot, waiting for what was to come next. The Cook settled, the steam cleared, they all stared. There was nobody there. Before they could gasp, before they could guess, the surface broke again and a figure appeared. Not the Beggar, nor yours truly. It was the Prince, not even wet, not even sorry, not even delighted. "Where's the ball?" was all he managed. "Where's the ball?"

And where was the ball? you might well ask — or, for that matter, the Beggar? Or, most urgent, where was I? Of ball and Beggar, I cannot speak. Of myself, the rest is odds-bod and strange to tell. I was no longer a flea, I was no longer anything. An idea. Moving through mist, moving through air. I liked being me better than a hare, a hare better than a flea, a flea better than this. I was above the palace, swirling, an element, nothing more. Until a sudden drop, hurtling down, the ground rushing up to meet me . . . oooooooooooooh!

My wife walked along the path to greet me as I shook myself and looked around me. There were my hands, there were my feet, here was my face, my coat, my breeches, my terrace, my wife—all my bits about me. I'd been dreaming. None of this had happened. I'd been dreaming. "I've been dreaming!" I told my wife, who smiled her sweet smile and ruffled my hair while I sighed the longest sigh you can imagine. Imagine it and it was twice that long. Then I heard a march and a clatter of armor and turned to see the King's Guards approaching. "His Majesty wants his story," said one, and my heart sank. What could I do? I had no story. I looked at my wife. I gazed into her river eyes, her lake eyes, her tender eyes, and whispered a goodbye. I never saw her again.

"It approaches the midnight and I've heard no story," said the King, sitting on his throne, the Queen beside him, the Prince in front, the court behind. "Do you remember the conditions?" "I do," I muttered, fear muddling my thoughts. "Well?" continued the King sternly. "Have you a story to tell or not?" I couldn't think. All I knew was that the day had gone, the last day—if only I hadn't gambled, if only I hadn't fallen asleep, if only this, if only that. One story more and there I'd be, released, intact, in clover.

The King drummed impatiently. The Cook stepped forward, glee bulging his eyeballs. "He hasn't, sire," he chortled, rubbing his fat hands, those hands I'd dreamed singed and unfingered. "He doesn't have a story, the pig, let me have him!" I shuddered. The Prince bobbed up and down until I wished him back on the ceiling. "Is there going to be a boil?" he asked his father, his smile terrifying. "I haven't got a story, sire," I admitted, and the court fell silent as I began my sorry tale.

"Let me tell you what happened to me today. I woke up, it was the last day of our agreement, my wife lay beside me, the sun streaming in, never was a man so happy, and then . . . and then I just couldn't think of a story, not a single one, and so I went out into the gardens and then things began to go very wrong. First of all I met a Beggar . . ."

And so I told the King of my adventures, of hares and fleas and mysteries, the worst day of my life, my wife's cruelty, the boiling oil . . . and what a tale it was, my dearies, how the tears coursed down my cheeks and the King's and the Cook's and the court's. And when at last I finished, there was a silence. A terrible silence. I bowed my head and resigned myself to what must surely follow. "And so, Majesty," I said, sad and woeful, "you see why I have no story to tell." The King blew his nose, the Queen mopped her tears with her handkerchief, tiny drops of water ran into my mouth and splashed my boots. So I stood until, finally, the King spoke.

"But that is the best story I ever heard," he said, his lips quivering. "And me," said the Queen, nodding. "And me," sniffed the Cook. I looked up. I looked about me. Suddenly the whole court stood and cheered and clapped my back and made me say again from start to finish the best story they'd ever heard, and then I understood what the Beggar had done. He'd given me a story. When I was a story short, he'd made me one.

As for my wife, she went off with the Beggar. She was enchanted, I think, otherwise it would have been cruel to have kissed him so, to have made me a flea. No, she was under his spell. Definite. And still is, I suppose. She was so taken by his magic, she set off in search of him. I never saw her to this day. She was a lovely. Lovely red hair. As for the Cook, he threw out the pot of oil, and kept the stone instead. Whenever a poor unfortunate came a-begging, he would make them the most delicious soup. And they would go on their way with a full belly, telling of a kind Cook who could make soup from a stone.

So that is how a story was lost and then found. And is still told to this day, for the King will hear no other. Only it's changed now. The wife comes back to the Storyteller. The Storyteller becomes King. You know how it is in stories. . . .

A NOTE ON THE TYPE

The text of this book was set in Garamond No. 3, a modern rendering
of the type first cut by Claude Garamond (c. 1480–1561). Garamond
was a pupil of Geoffroy Tory and is believed to have based his letters on
the Venetian models, although he introduced a number of important
differences, and it is to him we owe the letter which we know as "old
style." He gave to his letters a certain elegance and a feeling of
movement that won for their creator an immediate reputation and the
patronage of Francis I of France.

Composed by The Sarabande Press, New York, New York
Printed and bound by Mandarin Offset, Hong Kong
Design by Virginia Tan.   Layout by Irva Mandelbaum